D1608231

THE CURVY GIRL RESCUE

DISASTER CITY SEARCH AND RESCUE

GINNY STERLING

INTRODUCTION

Matt Jackson never expected being a police officer would give him wings… and an angel!

When bombs went off while on duty, he was thrown well over ten feet in the air, waking to the most wonderful dream a man could wish for! His nurse was a curvy bombshell with an incredible smile and a personality that matched his own. Even his K-9 dog, Barbie, adores the gorgeous nurse smuggling in homemade doggie treats.

Alice Chadwick was a just an ordinary girl. A nurse, fur-baby momma, and wannabe chef, her schedule gives her little time to find that *someone special*. When the gorgeous officer flirts as she's taking his vitals, she isn't sure what to make of him. He's got a snarky sense of humor, making her laugh more during her twelve-hour shift than she had in years.

Perhaps Officer Jackson bumped his head a little harder than anyone thought, or was he just a brutal tease toying with her heart?

For every quip, every joke, Alice had a witty comeback that left him yearning for more—even after she refused to go out with him. When fate intervenes and it's up to Matt to rescue his damsel-in-distress, will his luscious lady-love realize that maybe he's not such a bad guy after all?

Step into the world of Disaster City Search and Rescue, where officers, firefighters, military, and medics, train and work alongside each other with the dogs they love, to do the most dangerous job of all — help lost and injured victims find their way home.

This one was for me...
I loved the flirtation between Matt & Alice and I hope you enjoy
their story as much as I did.

❧

Ginny Sterling Newsletter

CHAPTER 1

"THIS IS *NOT* WHAT I SIGNED UP FOR…"

Officer Wright muttered under his breath as he stood beside his fellow officers, there on the streets of Dallas. This was a fiasco, a joke, a big fat celebrity media event that always ended up in a mess. Every time that they were assigned to 'help direct traffic' at one of these exhibitions, someone ended up in an accident, hurt, or worse.

… And to Matt Jackson, this was not what he signed up for either. He just wasn't dumb enough to voice it aloud.

Both men had spent years training and honing their skills. Matt was ex-Army and had landed a prime spot on the police force in one of the biggest metropolitan cities near the small town he grew up in. Living in the suburbs of Dallas, it was a rare event to go 'into the big city'… and now it was a daily humdrum.

The fascination with the city was gone. The awe of seeing Reunion Tower lit up at night, the massive skyscrapers outlined with a neon green light, the twisting winding highways dubbed the 'Mixmaster' but internally called 'the blender' because of the horrific accidents they'd all worked over the years.

He knew he was jaded—and nothing would return that innocence once gone.

"Suck it up, Wright," Matt growled, sick of listening to his best friend whine. They were all hot, all tired and over-worked, standing there at attention in full gear. They were prepared for anything—except this.

He would have felt better if someone was telling him that some rock star was putting on a performance, because then they'd know how to handle the crowd. No, this was going to be a mess and bring out the weepy-tissue-hugging-plate-collecting ladies from who-knows-where... it was also going to bring out the 'crazies'.

Royalty in town was a disaster of epic proportions. The city would grind to a halt for the slew of shutterbugs and paparazzi that would literally trip over each other to get a snapshot of some fancy prince or princess with food on their shirt or an eyelash out of place.

... And the 'crazies'...?

They were scarier.

Fake makeup, wigs, t-shirts, sobbing and pulling at them-selves in an effort to get noticed... those were the milder version. The psychotic ones who were dangerous were either obnoxiously screaming 'I love you!' and trying to throw themselves bodily over the barricades... or silently waiting for their chance.

The silent ones terrified him.

"You are the same as the rest of us at this moment," Matt grunted, hooking his thumbs in his belt, scanning the area through black sunglasses. "We get a call to action—we come. You don't get to sit around waiting for the fun stuff."

"See, Jackson? That is where you are *soooo* wrong about me," Abel smarted off with a smirk and a wink. "You imagine that I'm better than everyone else- when in fact- it's the simple truth. Isn't that right, Barkley?"

Matt laughed at the outlandish statement, looking at the massive Bulldog beside Abel... who grinned at him knowingly.

Barkley was named after the dog on Sesame Street and was just like him in personality. Friendly, outgoing, quiet, and didn't have an enemy in the world. Definitely not the typical dog a police officer would have with him.

Abel had brought along Barkley several times with him on a few cases—much to the chagrin of his chief. The dog was absolutely not a K-9 animal in any way, shape, or form. He drooled, had a pushed-up nose that caused him to snort and snore, and little, short legs that would never catch a criminal on the run... but Barkley had other charm.

He was excellent with people.

Not his Barbie-girl.

Barbie, his seventy-pound German Shepherd, was all muscle and teeth to anyone she didn't know. He kept her on a tight leash and already had one warning on file regarding the dog. She bit—and hard.

Matt had been the recipient several times until he established dominance. He literally wrestled the massive dog to the ground and held her until she gave in. Training Barbie had been a nightmare. The dog was just about as pig-headed as he was.

In fact, Barbie was waiting in the car right now because Matt knew this would be a sensory overload for his furry partner... and in moments of trouble, he couldn't afford to be dragged down the streets by a hysterical purebred machine that spotted a new 'toy' to attack.

"So, who do you think it's going to be? What mysterious royal are we getting?" Matt asked, glancing over at his car that contained Barbie. Away from the world, once they were home and she felt comfortable, the massive animal was a teddy bear. She was his best friend, his partner, and favorite window-licker in the world…

"I don't know, but I wish they'd have told us," Abel quipped. "I would have bought one of those porcelain plates with their faces on it just to get an autograph. Can you imagine? What if it's like someone really freakin' famous? Like Princess Margaret or Fergie?"

"Fergie… as in the singer?" Matt asked, looking at Abel in surprise.

"No! Sarah Ferguson. Geez, don't you even read the trash magazines?"

"No?" Matt laughed. "I watch *real news* and stay away from that gossip stuff."

"Real news makes me feel like I take my work home with me. I like to laugh, and some of the stuff they put out there in that 'gossip stuff' is a real hoot."

"I'm sure it's probably someone big, because of how much of the city they assigned us to watch. Did you see the map on the board? The city is being patrolled all the way down from Walnut Hill Road to Lemmon Avenue, and clear over to Skillman Road. I'm telling you—this isn't an insignificant event."

"No. I know. It's a waste."

"Why is that? Look at all the people lining up on this road. I've never, ever, seen so many smiling faces on Mockingbird Lane. They are all waiting to glimpse some mysterious *'peer of the realm',*" Matt jeered, "…who will do nothing but wave, smile, and then disappear two seconds later."

"Exactly. A waste of our time and the taxpayers' money."

"Hey. I like a free day of standing around doing nothing. It sure beats getting shot at for wearing a uniform in the wrong part of town."

"Not all of Dallas is like that."

"Nope—just my territory," Matt quipped.

His grandmother insisted on living in the same house she'd raised her children in, no matter how bad the area got... so as any dutiful grandson would do in his shoes? He volunteered to patrol his grandma's neighborhood.

"How is your grandma doing anyhow?" Abel asked.

"She's a stubborn ol' bat," Matt sighed heavily. "I love her to death, but I really wish she'd move. It's only getting worse too - all the time. Last weekend there was a murder in the streets—*on the very street she lives on* - her street. Some cop I was... sheesh!"

"What do you mean?"

"How threatening and protective do I actually look if I am standing there yelling, '*Grandma go back inside—Now!*' at the top of my lungs?"

Matt had for sure thought that he was going to lose Barbie or come upon her in the midst of a slaughter like she had gone rabid. It was a horrific scene, nearly giving him heart failure...

His grandmother was screaming out into the yard, waving her little weathered fist like she was some heavy-weight wrestler instead of the ninety-pound woman that barely came up to his ribs.

Barbie had shot off like a rocket into the dark after some-one. The drug-sniffing dog had caught the scent and lost her ever-lovin' mind...

He had to get approval to use a different leash after she snapped that nylon piece of junk that day.

"I see what you mean."

"Dude—you don't understand how stubborn she is either! My own grandma gave me the finger and threatened not to make me any cookies on my birthday. She's fierce and scary!"

...Almost as scary as Barbie on a bad day, Matt smiled to himself at the thought of the two of them in the ring.

"That's harsh, man," Abel chortled in delight.

Just then, a roar of excitement seemed to spread down the street as the radios on their shoulders crackled in alert.

"10-17 to your location."

"Copy that," Matt radioed back quickly.

"10-30. Do you copy? 10-30 team. High threat."

"10-30?" Abel mouthed curiously at him before joining in. Matt rolled his eyes, praying that Abel remembered the codes.

"Copy that—10-30. We are on alert. Any info?" Abel interjected.

"Negative. Dispatch is monitoring feeds and will report when we have more."

"Copy."

"Update— 10-58. Empty roads and detour traffic immediately from Mockingbird and Hillcrest. Do you copy? Clear it now, team!"

"We copy," Abel nodded, looking at him. "Let's go. That's us."

People were surging into the streets past the barricades that had been set up. Matt moved quickly, rushing forward to help contain some of the chaos. Both men began barking out orders to clear the road.

"Move it, people! Get behind the barriers!"

Dispatch never called a 10-30 unless there was a high security threat in the area. It could mean anything, too. It could be a report of a gun in the area, a break-in, one of the 'crazies' trying to reach the limo... anything that could be perceived as a threat to a person's safety.

Then, to his shock and horror—the procession stopped in the road.

Matt cursed fluently.

He was really glad Barbie was in the car—and prayed that she didn't lose her mind and shatter the rear passenger window with her enthusiasm. Things were about to go from bad... to much, much worse.

Abel seemed to understand that. His friend and fellow officer yanked up his radio off his shoulder and started barking out information into the mic...

"10-18. 10-18—all cars have stopped on the road. Do you copy?"

"10-9—say again?"

"I repeat—all cars have stopped. The doors are opening. 10-20 at Mockingbird and Hillcrest... *ohhhh nooo...*"

Matt turned in alarm at Abel's words, his back to the cars as he tried to contain the people leaning over the barricades. He rolled his eyes as he realized that 'bad-to-worse' just turned into 'nuclear' and the people before him were going to have an utter meltdown...

Even Abel was stammering as a tiny blonde-haired woman exited the vehicle in a white pants suit, immediately followed by a middle-aged woman in a dark skirt and blouse. Four massive men got out of the middle vehicle, lining up behind the woman in white.

She smiled and began waving to the crowds.

"Uh... 10-33? I think?" Abel said weakly into the mic.

"Say again?"

"Um—she's out of the car and walking in the street, waving," Abel repeated numbly, unable to tear his eyes from the woman. *This* was the mysterious royal that was visiting North Texas and Officer Wright was practically drooling on himself at the sight of her.

Matt cleared his throat loudly, spurring the man into action.

"10-33 to my location," Abel ordered quickly as the woman walked towards the barricades fearlessly. "10-33 immediately! The... the... um... royal, queen, princess, whatever she is… she's heading into the crowd. I repeat, we are going to need more men here—*quickly!*"

The crowd swarmed, surging towards where the location of the woman in white was standing, shaking hands, and smiling at people. Cameras were clicking, people had out their cell phones, and the media was racing down the sidewalks to get a video of the woman working the throng of people up into a fierce frenzy.

"Miss? Ma'am? Your majesty…?" Abel stammered, looking all tongue-tied and googly-eyed. If he had pink puffy hearts floating around his head with little cherubs, Matt wouldn't have been surprised in the slightest.

"We need to get her more security. She needs to go inside until more police arrive," Matt barked out, pushing against the people that were trying to climb over the barricades now. They were making it into the streets and the chaos was overflowing.

Someone was going to end up hurt!

"Is something the matter?" a soft voice said in perfect English.

"You-you need to get to safety," Abel stammered.

"Is something wrong, officer?"

She was smiling at Abel, and his brain was obviously melting… about to leak out of his ears at any moment. Matt couldn't help the groan of annoyance that escaped him, but neither heard him.

"Stupid idiots," he muttered.

The duo was having a chit-chatty conversation there in the middle of the street, surrounded by people who would pay for a lock of the fancy princess' hair.

Abel needed to use the brain in his head, not the one in his pants, to get them all out of this mess… not asking Princess-Pretty-Pants what her favorite color was.

"OFFICER WRIGHT!" Matt barked, angling his head

pointedly in an effort to tell him silently to get her royal-frou-frou inside. He didn't give a flip what her name was or what color she liked...

His target needed to get to cover... NOW.

Abel snapped back to attention as the woman's paid goons shooed her into a building. The crowd seemed to deflate down to a minimal roar... and he was relieved. Matt looked back at his car to see that Barbie was still contained inside, but there was foam on the outside of the glass.

Smiling, he could only imagine the teeth prints or scratches she would have left on the door panel and seats in her attempt to get free in order to 'play'...

"I hope that was the craziest part of the day," Matt whispered aloud, as he returned to his position directly in front of the hospital where the princess had disappeared inside for the media event.

EVERYTHING HAPPENED IN SLOW MOTION.

A faint pop from somewhere triggered every instinct within his body. Jackson turned to face the front of the building where he stood at the barricades, only to see something out of a movie unfurl before his eyes.

From inside the children's hospital that specialized in spine research, he saw a glowing orb floating towards the doors followed by a rush of heat... just seconds before he was lifted off of the ground.

A bomb, Matt thought wildly... and he was helpless to do anything. He could feel himself floating backwards like a feather, weightless, as the concussion blast carried him for what felt like forever, but he knew it would be only seconds before he died.

He heard another massive pop, but this time it was from

within his helmet as he struck the ground. Flashes of electric pain radiated down his entire body as everything went deathly still.

This is it... he mused faintly, tasting metal in his mouth.

He lay there, cognizant of what had happened but unable to move or focus. Everything hurt. Someone was touching him, touching his hand... but he couldn't open his eyes to see who it was yet.

Voices, faint and hollow sounding, like someone speaking from far away or underwater, were heard. It was all garbled, incomprehensible, and bothered him. Why couldn't he understand what they were saying?

Matt finally cracked open his eyes, wincing at the sunlight. Smoke was billowing out from somewhere nearby. He could smell it.

People needed help... heck, he needed help.

He tried to move, but couldn't seem to make things work right now. He knew he should stand up, help his fellow officers, and survey the wreckage after the bomb... but his limbs weren't willing to agree.

Barbie...

Where was his dog?

He was so glad he'd left her in the SUV safely. If she had been with him, she would have been blasted into the air, too.

"Hey man..." Matt heard a voice from a million miles away and saw a figure enter his line of view. Blinking slowly, he tried to acknowledge whoever the fuzzy figure was and couldn't make his voice work.

He opened his mouth a few times, blinking, trying to draw everything into focus. His head was aching so badly— and he was so dizzy that he might vomit.

"You okay?" the muffled voice said.

Matt tried again. This time he knew he got the words out because that silhouetted figure nodded.

Nods were good... he thought wildly.

He wasn't going to try it, but nods were definitely easier to understand right now rather than that weird underwater-gibberish he was trying to decipher.

... And why did his nose itch right now?

He wanted to smile, to joke around, but nothing was working. Sleep was calling to him and he was afraid to close his eyes, but helpless against it.

It was Abel beside him, he realized faintly.

Abel was talking to him... and talking wayyyy too fast. He tried to raise his hand to stop him but could only manage to get a finger off the asphalt... maybe?

"Bleeding too, buddy. That was a heckuva blast. The ambulance is on the way."

He wanted to tell him he was okay, but couldn't hardly move. It was like he was shell-shocked... and someone was ringing a bell nearby or he was losing his mind. He wanted to ask a bunch of questions, tell Abel to check on others because he would be okay, but nothing came out.

Nodding was still good, right?

Matt nodded slowly, wincing.

Nodding was bad.

VERY bad.

Oh, mercy. The world was spinning, and he was going to vomit. If he couldn't nod, did that mean he would choke to death right there in the streets if he puked?

... And Abel was still talking.

Did the man ever shut up?

"Keep Barkley with you, okay?"

Matt must have said something because Abel replied before getting to his feet. Where was he going?

Now he heard bells and sirens?

Did that mean the Waaaa-mbulance was on the way?

He realized he was a jerk in that moment because he

always thought people were so needy when they were about to get aid, dubbing the ambulance the 'waaa-mbulance'... but he understood that basic, guttural need for hope.

... because he needed help and could use a large dose of hope, too.

He lay there on the asphalt, trying to remain coherent and praying that they would get to him in time. Head trauma could be deadly and there was no telling what else was affected on him. He was trying to take stock of his condition, and nothing was functioning right now. He just prayed he wasn't paralyzed.

Matt wiggled his finger again... or at least tried.

He could feel that inky blackness pulling at him and knew that if he fell asleep, he might not wake up. He needed something for the sheer, mind-numbing pain that he was in... and the comfort that would come knowing that whoever helped him, held his very life in their hands.

CHAPTER 2

"ALICE, YOU LUCKY GIRL," MONIQUE TEASED AT THE NURSES'
station as she flipped through her chart. "You've got a live
one in room 912. They've had to sedate him three times
already. He keeps waking up and asking for his Barbie-girl.
Nut-jobber, if you get what I'm sayin'…"

"912? Isn't that the police officer that they brought in
yesterday afternoon?"

"The same."

"Oh," Alice let slip. "I'm so sorry to hear that. Head injury,
right?"

"Yep—and some yahoo thought it would be funny to
bring in Cujo and tie it to his hospital bed. We've got Animal
Control on the way, and it's so bad that even Stevens said
you can wait to do your rounds in there."

"Wait… there's a dog in there?"

"More like a tail with big teeth. I swear there was more
foam on that dog's mouth than what I use to shave my legs."

"Is the patient in danger?"

"No. She seems to be protecting him."

"Aww, that's sweet!"

13

Monique rolled her eyes in disbelief.

"Somehow, I knew you'd say that— and that is why they gave you Looney-Tunes for your shift. Because of the 'itty-bitty-puppers' that we all knew you'd brave dismemberment for to pet. It was a *joke*, Alice. No one wants you to even try to pet that snarling beast."

"She's probably just scared."

"Or rabid?! Seriously, Alice! Wait for Animal Control to get here."

Monique flipped her chart closed and picked up a tray before wrapping her stethoscope over her shoulders. Alice nodded, mimicking her and not saying a word as her mind raced.

She loved animals.

They gave her a measure of comfort that was irreplaceable. Animals gave affection unconditionally. They didn't talk back. Their primary goal in life was to sleep, eat, breath, love, and play... which seemed like a simplified version of what she wanted in her own life.

And to Alice?

Everything Monique was saying meant that there was a terrified poochie waiting to be snuggled upon and just needed a little love and affection.

Maybe she was a fool, and maybe the animal was indeed rabid... but it wouldn't hurt to take a peek and give up half of her ham sandwich she brought for lunch in the process.

She could stand to lose a few pounds, anyhow...

Inspired, Alice tucked the chart under her arm and disappeared into the lounge to retrieve her sandwich. As she dug it out of her insulated bag, she heard a few knowing snickers behind her. She straightened up just in time to hear Marjorie's voice.

"How's your diet going, Alice?"

Hateful creature!

"The same as yours, Marjorie," she smiled sweetly, taking a bite of the sandwich with a flourish before walking out of the lounge.

So, she wasn't a fashion model and truthfully, she didn't care.

After seeing all sorts of people come and go in the trauma unit of the emergency room, Alice focused on her health – not the number on the scale. It was people like Marjorie that labeled her eating healthy as a 'diet' and mocked her every chance she got.

Walking down the hallway, she had the chart tucked under her arm and the ham sandwich suspiciously hidden in her scrub pocket, praying she didn't get any Dijon on the fabric. It would leave an oily spot that would be a pain to remove in the wash.

—As she neared the door, she heard the rumbling growl from within, warning her. Pressing on the handle, the door gave almost silently, and Alice felt like she was entering the lair of some angry demon...

The massive German Shepherd was staring at her with large black eyes.

That would be said demon, she mused.

The muzzle of the animal was curled upwards, revealing sharp canines that could tear or shred... but it was the dog's cursory look at the man on the hospital bed that was the giveaway.

"Poor sweetie! This guy is your furdaddy, isn't he?" Alice whispered gently, kneeling beside the door. She didn't want to be perceived as a threat, but rather as a friend.

"He's gonna be okay and I'm fine with you staying so long as you don't decide that I'm lunch. We can be besties and help him together."

The animal swung its deadly glare back at her and specks

of spittle fell onto the floor as she licked her chops menacingly.

"Do you smell that, sweet girl?" Alice asked, pulling out the sandwich. She broke off a piece and threw it on the floor close to the dog. The massive canine immediately inhaled it in one bite and looked at her expectantly, those teeth still gleaming in the dim light provided by the single lamp behind the hospital bed.

"Hmm?" she asked, gesturing again with a piece of the sandwich. "I'm here to help, not hurt."

Alice tossed another piece, and the dog looked at her inquisitively, angling her head to the side... but no longer baring those teeth at her. The rumbles were still coming from her chest, but she was more curious than upset at the moment.

Alice edged forward slightly, before tossing another piece down.

The Shepherd sat, mimicking her, watching, and leaving the food untouched... almost as if they were at a standoff, measuring each other for the possibility of a threat.

"I'll make you a deal," Alice said softly, talking to the animal like she could understand her. "You let me get his vitals and pet you—and you'll get the rest of the sandwich I have - plus you'll get to stay with your furdaddy. If you bite me, it won't be pleasant. I will freely admit that I will ugly-cry something fierce."

The rumblings in the animal stopped.

"That's my good girl," Alice crooned gently. There must have been something in her tone because the dog lay down on the floor and looked up at the bed, whining at the man.

She felt tears burn in her eyes as she realized the massive dog was indeed very protective of the man. She loved her furdaddy, and didn't understand what was going on.

"Poor baby," she said thickly, holding out the sandwich

and offering up a little prayer that her finger didn't get eaten either. A large pink tongue snatched it off her palm and inhaled it in a single bite.

Alice chuckled.

"That was honey-baked ham, and you should have at least tasted it," she teased, reaching forward again, tentatively, allowing the dog to smell her hand. Several tense moments passed as the muzzle got extremely close to her, sniffing, before whining again.

Reaching over, she began to scratch her ears, pet her head, and cradled her muzzle in her hands.

"I understand, sweetie. I have furbabies too. My girls love some little treats. How about you be a good little poochie and let me check his vitals? I promise to run home during my lunch and bring you back some snackies, okay?"

"Alice, you are utterly insane..."

Monique's voice was the barest whisper from behind her, causing Alice to tense as the dog became alert of the new intruder.

"Shhhh..." Alice crooned, petting the animal again. "Monique, shut the door and tell Animal Control they aren't needed. She's just scared and concerned for him. It's all under control and they just need to be left alone."

"If someone comes in here, she'll bite them."

"He's an officer, right? This is a K-9 animal and they need to be left alone, regardless. Put someone outside the room or a sign on the door, that way they feel protected."

"The hospital isn't going to go for that. We are a trauma unit – not a kennel."

"If Animal Control takes her, they will put her down for being dangerous. Would you harm an officer deliberately?"

"No."

"Neither would I... and she's just as much of a police officer as this unconscious man is. Now, please. Call

17

Animal Control and close the door so she will relax again...
Please."

As the door closed, the animal whined and nudged her
hand again, wanting more affection. She heard the jingle of
the dog tag and picked it up, smiling, before blowing kisses at
the animal.

"Well hello, Barbie. I guess your furdaddy isn't crazy after
all, is he? He was just asking for his pretty girl and very
worried about you," she chuckled as the animal licked her
face. "Yep, I snuck a bite before you got my sandwich."

Alice looked up from her seat on the floor and looked at
the bed for the first time. The dark-haired man was
bandaged heavily around his head with a shadowy growth on
his jaw. He looked to be quite heavily sedated, sleeping
soundly.

"Now, a promise is a promise," Alice muttered softly. "I
need to check on him and run home to get you some treats.
Be a very good girl so you can stay with him, Barbie. Okay?"

She got up and slowly approached the bed where the man
slept, anticipating the animal to get upset again. Instead,
Barbie watched her closely without blinking. Checking his
pulse, oxygen levels, and blood pressure, she turned back to
the dog.

"See? All done," she replied. "Now, I'm going to finish my
rounds and return with snackies for my new favorite Barbie-
girl."

The large dog let out a soft woof of agreement before
laying down on the cool linoleum floor again. She was back
to guarding her partner, who remained unaware of what had
just transpired.

Alice smiled, slipping out the door silently.

CHAPTER 3

ALICE WAS TAKING A FEW MOMENTS TO PET BARBIE AND RELAX away from the rest of the chaos during her lunch break the next day. She had brought plenty of leftovers and had split it with the animal.

Today was a salmon patty, whole grain rice, and steamed broccoli... to which the dog never blinked an eye as she devoured the entire thing in a few heaping breaths.

She was currently feeding Barbie a homemade dog treat that she had made yesterday after work for Ginger and Snoopy, her own two dogs. Barbie put a massive paw on her leg and laid her head down on her lap, pushing against her stomach. The animal really was a push over once she trusted you.

"Awww, my sweet girl," Alice crooned. "You like your ears scratched just like my little Snoopy, don't you?"

"Her belly, too."

A gravelly voice echoed in the silence, as Alice looked up to see that the man was awake.

Barbie jerked her head away and jumped onto the

hospital bed, making him grunt in pain for a second as the massive animal immediately lay prostrate across him, nuzzling him.

It was such a sweet, tender moment that Alice immediately wiped away tears and sniffed. The big, scary animal had quite a tender spot for this mysterious police officer.

"Take it easy, doll," he chuckled painfully. "I'm alright unless you finish me off."

Alice got to her feet and grabbed his chart, jotting down notes. She glanced at the machines and walked to the side of the bed to check his vitals.

"Tell me you are here for my daily sponge bath," he teased, closing his eyes and wincing.

"I don't think so," Alice chuckled. "And I've heard that line before."

"Hourly, then?" Matt quipped, cracking open an eye and watching her.

"I'm here to take your vitals."

"Please tell me my temperature is included... please?"

"Of course," she smiled at the flirtatious tone in his voice.

"Rect..."

Alice shoved the thermometer in his mouth sweetly without a word. His eyes widened at the forcefulness she used before he chuckled with delight, causing the corners of his eyes to crinkle with humor.

She knew she had about sixty-to-ninety seconds to prepare for the next onslaught of flirtation from this handsome man.

While she waited, she petted Barbie again – causing his eyes to widen as he looked between her and the dog. The large tail thumped happily on the bed as she moved a paw, to include Alice in the bodily hug that was sprawled across the patient right now.

"How are you feeling?" Alice asked, watching the clock as she counted, checking his pulse.

He pointed at the thermometer knowingly.

"I know—and you are almost done."

Seconds later, the thermometer buzzed, and she plucked it out of his mouth, shooting the plastic cover into the trash receptacle beside the bed with practiced ease.

"Ninety-eight," she announced. "Are you sore? Hungry?"

"A little of everything," he smiled in acknowledgement. "We could have a Jell-O cup together and call it a date? You can play nurse all you want, kiss all the boo-boos better... including the one on my head."

Alice gave him a deadpan look.

"Let me guess which one... because I've heard that nasty pickup line too, officer."

She couldn't help the smile that touched her lips as he burst out laughing at the raunchy punchline that was obviously on the tip of his tongue. Wincing, he tried to stop laughing as both hands flew to his head and cradled it protectively. He laid back in the bed, closing his eyes, and taking several deep breaths.

Alice leaned forward and spoke softly, not wanting to hurt him any further. She flashed a penlight to make sure his pupils were dilating. He flinched and closed his eyes again.

She imagined his head was pounding insanely from the pressure within it. A concussion and slight skull fracture were no laughing matter. He was a lucky man to be alive.

"Maybe you should let yourself heal first, Officer Jackson," she breathed.

His eyes opened at that moment, staring into hers. Deep brown met her hazel ones and held fast. Alice's breath caught in her throat as she realized that he wasn't just handsome... he was devastatingly so.

"Rest," she ordered faintly.

"That wasn't a 'no' to our Jell-O date," he uttered quietly, as if the words hurt his head to say aloud. "I bet you like cherry. Tell me you are a cherry girl…"

"I prefer lime with cool whip on top."

"Gosh, I love a wild-child…" he breathed, looking utterly fascinated—and exhausted.

"You should see my Saturday nights," she found herself teasing, flirting along as a blush crept up her cheeks. This was incredibly inappropriate and the most fun she'd had in forever.

He wasn't about to stop, either.

Alice leaned back from where she'd hovered to check his pupils, only to have him touch her hand where it rested on the stainless-steel bars of his bed. The warm, electric touch of his hand jolted her to awareness.

This was definitely wrong.

This was how reports got filed, nurses got in trouble, and how you ended up on the news. She couldn't lose her job because of some officer that was an outrageous flirt and took things too far. No, she needed to get out of here.

"Hanging from the rafters in a sexy bikini, I hope," he breathed, smiling.

"Oh, you know it," she chuckled nervously, smiling as she quickly finished up her checks. "Wild-child extraordinaire, right here."

"So, you *are* free Saturday?" he asked quietly.

"But you aren't," she declined immediately, not sure when he was being released from the hospital, but this was a bad idea all the way around. She flipped open the chart blindly, backing away in retreat.

This was going too far, too fast.

"Nope, looks like you'll have all the fun. You're scheduled for a rectal exam to see if you are indeed an… "

Alice couldn't finish the joke because his laughter roared

to life... quickly followed by a whimpering moan of pain. She heard Barbie's sympathetic whine as the door closed and she felt the pang of guilt within her chest, knowing she'd caused him to hurt.

Leaning on the closed door, she caught her breath and tried to still her rapidly beating heart. She replayed the flirty conversation back in her mind, silently tickled by his quick wit... but also looking at it analytically if he filed a report claiming she was too forward with him.

This was a mess!

She would have to be candid with him, or find another nurse to befriend Barbie, just so he could be treated there without separating him from his furry partner.

"Oh, I'm in real trouble, my sweet Barbie-girl..." Matt breathed, trying to get control of the pain racing through his head.

He had opened his eyes to see the most delectable Angel of Mercy in his room, playing with his dog like she was a harmless little pooch. Those eyes, that smile, that curvy body... it was killing him in the most pleasant way possible.

He meant it when he asked her out for Jell-O...

Good gravy, he'd give up his entire meal tray if it meant he got to look at her for another ten minutes. She was so incredibly gorgeous! He'd watch paint dry if it made her smile at him.

Maybe he was just as bad off as Abel was when he spotted Princess-Fancy-Pants strutting around...

Matt covered his eyes and groaned at the realization, before pushing the button to shut off the light bar that was making his head ache even more.

His evening nurse was the exact opposite of his Angel of the Morning.

Where his angel was fearless, this one was mean. She threated to muzzle Barbie, knock her out, or call Animal Control... all of which just pissed off Matt to the point that his head was aching again.

He ended up hollering for the strange nurse to get out of his room - and demanded that someone fetch his 'pretty angel', before he started seeing spots again behind his closed eyes. He was madder than a firecracker at the way they were all acting like Barbie was some wild beast...

She was trained to take down anyone that was a threat to him and sniff out drugs. How could she be blamed for doing only what she was trained from birth to do? He had raised that wriggling fat puppy from the moment she breathed in for the first time.

He heard Barbie's growl before the door opened to his room.

"Mr. Jackson, how are you feeling?"

"Pretty peeved, right now."

"Can we get you anything?" the man asked from the door- way, refusing to enter the room—and that was probably best for everyone.

"Who was my nurse this morning?"

"I'm not sure. I'd have to check."

"Well, *that's* what you can get me... and then leave me alone."

"Are you hurting?"

"Not enough to continue this conversation 'cause it is giving me a heckuva headache," he snarled. "Get my other nurse and I'll talk to her."

"Mr. Jackson..."

"Nope," he said stubbornly, shutting off his light again. "Done talking."

"Shall I get the doctor?"

Matt didn't even deign to answer. He didn't need the doctor or any other medicine. He needed rest… and to know more about the woman that fascinated him.

CHAPTER 4

ALICE GLARED AT THE PHONE SLEEPILY AS THE BRIGHT LIGHT OF the faceplate illuminated the space beside her bed. Ginger and Snoopy began barking at each other and raced out of the bedroom, assuming it was time to get up. She stared at the phone again, uncomprehending, and realized it wasn't her alarm going off…

It was a phone call.

"Mmhullo…"

"Alice, hey girl… were you sleeping?"

"It's three in the morning. Yes, of course I was sleeping," she grumbled, sitting up. "What's wrong."

"Your boy-toy in 912 is being a pain-in-the-patootie… refusing treatment unless you come and give it to him. What is it with you and wild animals?"

"One more time… but slowly. I need coffee if we are having a discussion. No coffee, no talkee," Alice ordered, getting up and stabbing at her robe several times before she finally got an arm in the sleeve. "He's doing what?"

"He is refusing anyone—and he's due for medication. His blood pressure is up 'cause he is fighting us on everything and grunting in pain. I'm sure it's causing pressure in his head to increase, but he won't…"

"He's hurting…?" Alice whispered.

"Yeah—and asking for you. I know you aren't scheduled until six, but we can swap shifts or something because I can't stand a patient to suffer."

"Neither can I."

"That's why we are the best at what we do, girl."

"Let me get dressed and I'll head in."

"I'll tell your lover-boy that you are on the way…"

"Don't call him that… and certainly don't say that around anyone else."

"You know I'm only teasing, right?" Monique retorted, and then grew quiet. "Unless something…"

"NO."

Alice got quiet. Neither woman said a word as they both sat there silent on the phone, unwilling to unpack the abrupt denial from Alice or the burning curiosity that now had to be racing thru Monique.

"I'll be there soon," she said and quickly ended the call.

AS SHE ARRIVED, several nurses looked at her in surprise and then checked the clock on the wall. Alice felt a horrible blush heating her cheeks because she knew she wasn't scheduled for another three hours or so.

Without a word, she plucked his chart from the wall and moved to the cabinet to withdraw his overdue medication.

"Has 912 eaten his dinner?"

"No, the dog ate it."

She wanted to smile at the waspish tone, but she also understood that the German Shepherd was pretty intimidating. She imagined that the tray was probably still in there too, licked clean by Barbie.

"Could someone get me a tray, then?"

"I'll have it waiting in the hallway."

"Perfect."

"You know, we shouldn't have to walk around on eggshells to help the man. That dog should be muzzled and sedated…"

"That *dog* is his *partner*…" Alice stressed, before softening her tone, "…and his friend."

"You are not thinking clearly."

"Probably not…," Alice shrugged. "I'm still waiting for my coffee to kick in."

Ignoring the curious stares, she walked down the hallway towards the officer's room. Before she even opened the door, she heard the growl, followed by a ragged moan of pain.

"Shhh, Barbie," Alice hissed quietly. "I'm here to help."

The room was dark, almost pitch black, except for the glow from the monitors beside the bed. She slowly walked in, a little afraid she would trip on something or worse. No one had taken the dog outside, and she knew that it was bound to have nature take its course soon.

"Officer Jackson, can you hear me?"

"Matt…" he whispered in the darkness.

"Look, we need to talk, but first you need to take some medicine and I need to take Barbie outside to go to the restroom."

"Head… hurts…"

"I know," Alice whispered, finally reaching the side of the bed. "Take this and keep the lights off. I will take Barbie out and be right back. She needs some care too."

"T-thank… you…"

"Of course."

Alice walked to the door and opened it, seeing several

eyes peering at her curiously. The tray of food was being carried down the hall towards the nurse's station.

"I'm going to take the dog to the restroom—but I need a clear path, so she doesn't get upset."

"You are bringing Cujo... *out here?*"

"Yes."

"I'm going to race her right out the side door and then I'll be back. Five minutes tops."

"And what are we supposed to do?"

"Hide," Alice grinned.

She shut the door, ignoring the comments and the cursing that was quick to follow from her announcement. She grabbed the dog's leash and got out a treat from her pocket, wrapping the leash around her wrist a few times.

"Please don't break my wrist," she whispered to the dog, patting it.

"She's... a good... girl," Matt whimpered, curled in a fetal position as he held his head painfully.

"I know. Rest, and I'll take care of her."

Within minutes, she returned and was quite surprised at how obedient the dog was. Apparently, Alice was now an honored part of her inner circle, because the dog didn't even try to escape. She listened and followed directions better than her own dogs.

Ginger would have bitten at the leash or tried to escape... and Snoopy? Well, she would have stopped every two feet to mark her territory in some fashion.

As she re-entered the room, she saw that Matt was uncurling just a bit and trying to relax. He wasn't moaning in pain anymore. Those tight abbreviated gasps from earlier were now relaxed breaths in the darkness.

"How are you feeling?"

"Better."

"Good," she replied, picking up the dirty tray and taking it out of the room. She reentered with a fresh tray and put it on the roll-around cart, brushing Barbie off the hospital bed where she lay at the foot, watching her. She knelt down and gave her a small doggie treat she made earlier in the evening, grateful she'd thought to do so...

"Let's get you fed so you don't get sick from the medication."

"Time... for our... Jell-O date?" he uttered softly.

"They were fresh out of lime," she smiled. "I'm going to turn on the lamp so you can see what you are eating, okay?"

"See... you," he corrected.

Alice flushed at the soft, gentle tone in his voice despite the pain. She turned on the light and looked over to see him watching her through cracked lids. A soft smile touched his unshaven face... he looked at her like she was the best thing that had ever happened to him.

"What's... your name, angel?"

It relieved her to hear his voice getting stronger with each passing moment. He needed more rest than he realized, but according to his chart, he was doing much better. If he continued on this path, he would be released in the next two days to go home and rest. With a slight fracture, there was nothing they could do but treat some of the symptoms and give the body time to heal.

He was lucky there wasn't more damage to his body other than the scrapes, bruises, and other things that came with falling abruptly on a hard surface.

"Alice."

"Ahh... how appropriate," he breathed, nodding. "I feel like I've traveled through the looking glass since the moment I woke up and saw you."

"You shouldn't say things like that," she replied almost immediately. "You need to eat and rest."

"I shouldn't say it, even if I happen to think it's true?"

"You could get me in trouble."

"And you could write your phone number down so I can call you when I get discharged. I already know your favorite things…"

"Knowing that I said lime Jell-O does not make you an expert on me."

"You're right," he agreed. "But agreeing to our first date would make it easier for us to have a second and third one."

"You are pushy, Officer Jackson."

"Matt," he corrected with a soft smile. "… and yes, I am."

"Is this why you made such a stink? To get me to come in so you could harass your way into asking me out?"

"No, angel…" he breathed softly, closing his eyes for a moment. "It's so I could just be near you and see your beautiful smile."

Alice sat back, reeling, unsure of what to say or do.

This was nothing she had ever expected. There was such a raw, genuine touch to his voice that she knew he wasn't teasing, but rather telling the truth, admitting that this was all to see her again.

She should be mad that he was carrying on like a toddler throwing a tantrum for not getting to play with his favorite toy - *her* - yet somehow, she was flattered beyond belief. No one ever really looked at her like that, and she had stopped trying to attract a boyfriend a few years ago.

She wore scrubs all the time, always wore a ponytail, and never wore makeup anymore. Nearing thirty, she had decided that she enjoyed being alone and the freedom it gave her. When she felt lonely, she had her furbabies to comfort her… and her cooking.

"Are you mad?" she finally asked after a moment. "I'm thinking you are insane, or that head bump was a little more severe than we originally thought."

"Just crazy about you."

"You don't even know me."

"But I'd like to... say 'yes' please."

"Yes, to what?"

"To our forever date..."

"You mean 'first'."

"Sure," he smiled wolfishly, looking utterly amused. That was when she realized he was apparently feeling much better.

"Were you faking?"

"No."

"I can't believe you," she snarled, hopping to her feet. "I actually felt bad that you were hurting and here you were goofin' around, trying to force me into actually falling for your corny lines..."

"My head did hurt—almost as much as my heart... but seeing you and taking that little pill, plus whatever just dosed automatically in the IV... well now... I feel freakin' amazing and a little dizzy."

"Are you still on pain meds?" she gaped, staring at the IV.

"You gave them to me. Correction: I'm a whole LOT dizzy now..."

"No – I meant... wait..."

Alice flipped open his chart and panicked.

He had now, officially, doubled up on his pain medication, which was a narcotic. Matt was higher than a kite... and soaring.

She uttered a curse word under her breath, because it was something she should have checked before dosing him—and who was the pharmacist on duty? It should have sent up a red-flag in the system showing he was already on something.

"You said a bad word..."

"I'm about to say a few more," she snapped, looking at the two of them, watching her carefully. "I'll be right back with the doctor."

"Barbie won't liiiike that," he sang out. "Have I mentioned just how unbelievably hot, and I mean H.A.W.T... I think you are? Mercy..."

"Great. I finally have a guy tell me I look hot, and he is in la-la-land because he's fully loaded on painkillers... and it only took a severe head wound to get there! Talk about flattery..."

"I feel sooooo sweepy..." he slurred, sagging on the bed.

Alice bolted out the door to get help... and get away from Matt.

CHAPTER 5

TWO DAYS LATER, AFTER BEATING HERSELF UP MENTALLY AND signing her safety incident report at the hospital, Alice was having to discharge the man who was quickly turning into her most prickly patient.

She had to give him credit—he was certainly persistent.

Thinking Matt had turned over a new leaf, willing to comply with hospital policies in order to get what he wanted, she realized it was all a ploy. He had obediently shut Barbie in the restroom to allow the doctor to check him. He ate his meals as ordered, was polite to everyone who checked on him, and it was all to lead to this moment.

"Guess what?" Matt asked the moment Alice walked in the room.

"What?"

"I'm being discharged today."

"I know—guess who is your discharge nurse?" she retorted, smiling at him.

He didn't say anything else, just smiling back at her.

Alice slipped Barbie a doggie treat from the house out of

her pocket, barely able to remove it from the Ziplock baggie before she snatched it happily.

"Alright, let's take your IV out and go over a few things."

"Yes ma'am," he said easily, his eyes dancing.

"What are you up to?" she asked cautiously.

"Nothing. I'm just trying to be a model patient for you."

Alice snorted.

"Okay, we'll do this your way," she sassed, ripping open an alcohol swap. The swabs helped take the tape off the patient's skin and prevented it from pulling terribly or ripping out any hairs.

Matt winced as she pulled slightly.

"Sorry," she muttered, concentrating, and swabbing a little more before lifting the tape again.

"Ouch!" he yelped.

"I'm trying," she began, scrubbing at the tape again and trying not to focus on how warm his arm was... or how muscular. Rippled muscles, veins, and deep tan skin made her breath catch in her chest.

"Keep trying," he grunted as she pulled at the tape.

"I am," she replied tautly, trying not to get upset. He was hurting, and she was supposed to keep from inflicting pain.

"Try a little harder," he ordered.

"Well, if you weren't so dang hairy, you big brute..." she snapped. "I wouldn't be waxing your 'ol stupid arm with the surgical tape!"

"Angel—I'm hairy all over!" he bit back.

Both sucked in their breaths and looked at each other. The tension was palatable in the room between them. He didn't look the slightest bit sorry for escalating things to an uncomfortable level...

No, she realized, he looked like he wanted to kiss her.

Matt opened his mouth for a second, hesitated, and then closed it.

35

Alice opened another alcohol packet, looking away from his piercing dark eyes. She could feel his eyes on her and knew he was watching for any sign of encouragement.

"I'm not trying to hurt you," she whispered, reaching for the tape.

His hand swatted her hand away, but before she could say anything or try to pull at the tape again? He grabbed the small, uplifted corner and yanked it off in one fell-swoop.

She heard his faint hiss of pain, followed quickly by a single grunt.

Looking up from his arm in stunned silence, she met his eyes and saw there were glassy. She knew from experience that tape could be excruciating, and joked in nursing school about her own 'waxing experience' in front of the other students.

"I could have kept swabbing at it," she began, only to see him yank the second tape strip off too, leaving dual red raw stripes on his tanned arm.

"Stop it, Matt!"

"Sometimes you just have to get past the uncomfortable part in order to get what you want done, finally," he mumbled. "I want to take you to dinner or whatever you want to do... but you and I are a thing—and I intend to show you that I'm the perfect guy for you, angel."

"No," she said softly, focusing on removing the IV now that it was exposed. The instrument slid out as he continued to talk, distracting her. *Gosh, why did his voice make her feel all jittery inside?* He had a beautiful timbre that would make her fawn for hours listening to him recite anything at all.

"You can say no if it makes you feel better, but I can tell you that I'm a good guy deep down, even if I'm a flirtatious jerk," he said gently, ducking his head to look at her. "I'm serious Alice."

"The answer is still no."

"Is there another guy? Are you into chicks?"

"What?" Alice balked, allowing blood to roll down his arm before she slapped the cotton ball on it. "Hold this!"

She quickly put tape on the cotton ball and folded up his arm.

"Keep pressure on it."

"I'm *trying* to keep pressure on it…" he teased quietly, watching her. "I'm *pressuring* quite a bit because I know after today, I might not see you again… and I'm just not okay with that."

"Officer Jackson…"

"Matt," he corrected immediately.

"Matt," she amended, "I don't feel it's appropriate for me to have any sort of friendship with someone I just spent the last few days taking care of at work. It just doesn't sit right— and I'm sure you understand having a code of ethics."

"Do I have to play in traffic to get you to spend time with me?" he smiled, watching her. "Because I absolutely will."

"No," she smiled at the outrageous comment.

"You say 'no' a lot lately."

"Because I have a reason to."

"Did I tell you I got my prescriptions already?" he said, suddenly changing subject and sitting back.

"You did?" Alice asked, confused.

She didn't see any prescriptions in his folder.

There were only the basic follow-up instructions. So long as he allowed himself to heal and touched base for a physical in a few weeks, he was released back to work in a month.

He pulled a slip of paper from the rolling table and handed it to her. Written on the prescription pad was his name, cell phone number, and an address…

"Just because this was completely unexpected doesn't mean that it should be ignored or avoided, Alice," he said gently.

Alice stared at it for several moments, her eyes watering with emotion.

This was so darn sweet, so clever and endearing, that it touched her heart. Where was this guy years ago when she was avidly searching for someone to fill her life? Now she had her little condo, her pups, and a world she'd slowly built for herself. She had carved out her little piece of heaven and was very protective of it.

"And before you say no again…" Matt continued, smiling wryly at her. "Just know that I can cook a mean spaghetti casserole—and my grandma likes to make my favorite peanut butter pie in return for having her only grandson visit. I always cook for my grandma on Sundays because that little woman can still put the fear of God in me sometimes…"

Alice looked up at the ceiling for several minutes, unwilling to wipe her eyes and needing to compose herself. He sat there quietly, as if he was giving her space to process it all.

"You don't have to answer now—but that will be a standing offer if you ever choose to call me in the future," Matt offered. "And I hope you do."

"Matt…"

"I will never make you regret it either," he interjected quickly before she could say anything else, causing her to sigh heavily. This was beyond tempting, and he was being so completely understanding about her hesitation.

… And what kind of man cooked for his grandma every week?

A good one! A keeper! that little voice whispered in the back of her head.

"I'll think about it," she hedged nervously.

"That's a vast improvement over you saying 'no,'" he smiled, nodding. The look of relief on his face was almost palpable.

"Thank you."

"I haven't said yes," she admitted, rolling her eyes.

"But you really want to, don't you?" Matt teased huskily in a hushed voice. "You know you want to meet my grandma and see dozens of embarrassing baby photos of me. I guarantee it will be cringe-worthy and you'll have a ball."

Alice couldn't help the chuckle that escaped her as she shook her head at his mischievous side. He just would not take no for an answer—and truthfully, she didn't really want to decline.

"Have I mentioned the peanut butter pie? It's amazing."

Barbie let out a whine and nudged her nose under Alice's hand.

"See? Even Barbie wants you to join us for dinner."

"That's pretty low," Alice whispered, patting the dog and trying not to look at Matt's handsome face. She was caving in, and was pretty sure the man had never been told 'no' a day in his life.

"I would scrape the bottom of the barrel if it meant you saying 'Yes, Matt! Let's go out on a date!" he admitted, in a falsetto voice.

"You sound like Mickey Mouse."

"I'll do every character's voice, if you'll just say yes…"

"You know you're begging."

"I'm a shameless fool when I know it's right and see utter perfection before me," he shrugged, smiling.

Alice got up from where she was perched and quickly gathered up the trash without looking at him. She haphazardly tucked the prescription into her pocket, remembering it had his phone number on it.

"Your things are in the locker," she said evasively and turned to pick up his chart, quickly moving to exit the hospital room. "I'll have someone bring a wheelchair in so we can roll you to the parking lot. Protocol. I'm sure you understand, and I believe there is an officer already waiting to drive you home."

"I'll see you Sunday, angel."

It was that confident wink that sent her fleeing out of the room – but only before he could hear her laughter bubble up from deep down inside.

The man was incorrigible… and she liked it a little too much.

SATURDAY EVENING, Alice found herself sitting in the break room alone and staring at the well-worn prescription. His handwriting was bold and aggressive… just like Matt.

The paper had been opened, folded, and re-folded about fifty times since he'd left the hospital three days ago. She had met no one quite like him—and part of her kept thinking it was a joke, some prank, that the team was playing on her.

Why would such a gorgeous man be interested in her?

Overworked, overweight, and having given up on finding someone to have a relationship with, she had moved on with her life. Her pups were her friends. She had her home and enjoyed her life… so why did it feel so empty now?

Picking up her phone, she began texting and stopped.

If she texted Matt, he would have her phone number and might call. Her break was over in ten minutes and she didn't have time to banter with him right now—no matter how tempting it might be to find out why he acted so interested while he was here… and could she take the letdown that was sure to come?

Alice sighed.

She slipped her phone back in the pocket of her scrubs and refolded the precious piece of paper once again. Never having been a person to jump to a decision, she had always given herself time to process. Being told 'Sunday' felt like a deadline—and she wasn't okay with being pressed for time.

Next Sunday would just have to do... and it might do him some good to be stood up for once in his life.

"MATT! Boy, put down your phone and get the rolls, honey, before they burn."

Matt flinched at the realization that his grandma was about to swat him on the hand with a rolled-up gossip magazine—and the rolls were actually burning. He was standing there in the kitchen mooning like some young boy who got his heart broken... not a grown man asking a woman over for dinner.

Alice wasn't coming.

"Grams, I wasn't gonna let the rolls burn," he said in a playful voice, rolling his eyes. "I like them suntanned—just like Leonardo DiCaprio in your magazine, like the one you are shaking at me..."

"Boy, don't you talk about my Leo—he's just far too pretty for words," his grandma sputtered, preening as she patted her hair, making him smile. His little grandma gave him a wink and moved to the table to make sure their place settings were correct.

He loved her to pieces and how strict she was when it came to family meals. Before his parents had passed, this was a family ritual. Every Sunday after church, everyone met at her house.

The table had fewer and fewer people every year, but was no less important. Structure, faith, and family had always been the Jackson-way... and Sundays were a treasure to him.

"C'mon Barbie," his grandma crooned at the big dog who was utterly mush before the woman. His mean, ornery

German Shepherd that made men cower in fear was literally pulling herself along the carpet as if she was scared of the five-foot-tall woman and begging for scraps of attention.

"That's my good girl," she crooned, slowly leaning forward to put a plate on the floor with some cooked chicken livers. His grandma spoiled Barbie unmercifully—just like Alice and the doggie treats. It made them both melt in her presence.

Alice had a good heart, and it showed.

Matt removed the rolls from the oven, plucking a few off the hot surface before blowing on his fingertips that were singed. He picked up the breadbasket and walked over to the table.

"Here you go, Grams... tanned just like your boy-toy!"

"I ought to tan your hide..." she smiled, making her wrinkles even deeper.

"But ya' love me, so you won't," Matt teased as she sat down.

He grabbed the chair and picked her up, scooting her forward to the table, before leaning down to kiss her on the cheek. The smell of powder and perfume always made him feel like he was still that ten-year-old boy that was so excited to get the privilege of sitting at the adults' table for Sunday supper.

"Love you, Grams."

"Sit down, you rascal," she ordered, patting his cheek before shooing him to his seat. "Maybe next time your friend can join us?"

Matt looked up to see her knowing smile. He opened his mouth for a moment, only to listen carefully to her next words...

"There's only one reason you would tell me you invited a friend to join us—and I can tell you, boy, that you need to give this girl space. You are the apple of my eye, but spoiled as all-get-out…"

"Now, Grams…"

She made a harsh noise that sounded like a buzzer, stopping him mid-sentence as she held up her hand.

"If you ask me, it shows mettle that she's letting you stew for a bit. I know you always want to charge headfirst into the thick of things, but you are going to have to be patient… and that isn't a bad thing to learn in your line of work. Now, are you saying grace—or am I? Because I'm hungry."

Matt chuckled and dutifully clasped his hands, bowing his head.

CHAPTER 6

IT TOOK ALICE ALMOST A MONTH TO GET UP THE NERVE TO actually text Matt. The moment she had, she regretted it instantly. He would never text her back or would tease her mercilessly about making him wait forever.

The telling moment had been last night watching television - alone.

She was slouched down on the couch, a dog on either side of her sleeping, with her favorite fuzzy blanket tucked up to her armpits. A bowl of ice cream was propped on her stomach as she indulged in some Blue Bell with Magic Shell on top.

It was her favorite outlet after a long, brutal week.

Tonight must have been the breaking point—or she was a hormonal mess, because normally movies didn't affect her quite so badly. She was watching a romance story when it hit her.

She was alone—and would forever be, if she didn't make some sort of effort. It was humbling to realize that her fear of things not working out guaranteed that they never would.

Then, in the movie... the main character died, leaving the

love interest with only her memories and a newly discovered pregnancy.

Oh, the sobbing was epic.

Alice had never felt so utterly eviscerated emotionally in her entire life. This character had loved—and lost—but had her memories and her child... while Alice had nothing.

She cried for the rest of the movie, finally having to turn it off.

There were wadded up tissues on the coffee table, the end table, and on her lap. Her ice cream was melted and milky, mixed with the tears of her emotional breakdown. It was causing her to practically choke.

She was so alone.

She had no memories but the single brief flirtations. There were no long, lingering kisses, no smiles, no tender moments... and certainly no baby.

A child had never been in the forefront of her mind—but seeing that movie, coupled with her wildly active imagination, she could picture that moment in some storybook fantasy built deep within her mind.

Alice craved a happily-ever-after of her own.

... And none of that would happen without even trying to take the first step of just saying hello and opening the lines of communication.

She'd picked up her phone, blindly texted through tears, and prayed that Matt didn't call because she was still sniffling wildly.

This might be a mistake—but she was willing to chance it for a moment of laughter and attention.

She clicked send—and re-read her text.

So, is the invitation still on? What should I bring?

"Ohmmmgee..." she breathed in growing horror, whispering aloud to herself. "That is so lame and assumptive. What is wrong with you, Alice?"

The phone screen darkened.

"Okay. I can go to Verizon and change my number—or I could lie and say it was a mistake, and I was texting someone else? The new phone excuse would work so long as he didn't call? Or I could tell him..." she blabbed in a panic, blowing her nose indelicately.

Her phone beeped.

"Oh, poop!" she hissed, picking it up right away and opening the screen.

Just bring that beautiful smile—and yes.

"Holy smokes... I have a date," she breathed, unsure if she should text back. Her phone had three dots appear, showing that he was typing something to her when another bubble of text appeared.

The best things are always worth waiting for... and I'm glad you texted.
See you tomorrow.

She couldn't help the tearful smile that touched her lips as she stared at the phone, picturing his face. This time, she felt a little more confident in her reply.

I'll see you tomorrow

"Jackson! Get off your stupid phone!"

Matt ducked down behind the door of his police cruiser as a volley of gunfire flew past them. His chief was behind another vehicle, looking absolutely astounded and furious that they had caught him on his cell phone in the middle of a shoot-out. The bullets and screaming curse words might be loud, but the ping of R2-D2 whistling in his pocket caught his attention immediately.

He only gave his personal cell phone number to very few people in this world—and his Grams was one of them… the other was Alice.

There might be 'crazies' in this world… but with the sound of that text, the rest of the world could wait. He'd immediately holstered his gun and pulled his cell phone from his pocket, illuminating his face in the darkness.

It was dumb.

Stupid.

… and highlighting exactly where he was hidden behind the car.

He didn't care because that chime told him it was urgent —and to him?

It absolutely was!

He'd been waiting for this text with bated breath for the last three or four weeks. A barrage of bullets wouldn't stop him from responding to either of those two women if they texted.

… And it was Alice.

He let out a whoop of joy and quickly texted back. Sitting there, among his shocked coworkers, he was having a personal conversation plopped on the asphalt with the occasional zing flying past him.

None of it mattered because he was going to see Alice again.

"JACKSON!"

He quickly slipped the phone in his pocket against his heart, grinning. Sunday couldn't come fast enough—and he sure hoped he didn't get shot or injured again. He still got headaches easily and wore a helmet much more than before because he was deathly afraid to knock himself hard enough to actually kill him this time.

"Sorry, sir. Emergency."

"We are having one ourselves, you know!"

"Yes, sir. On it."

Jackson listened as they received their orders. He couldn't help the foolish smile that stayed on his face—and within his heart. Tomorrow he would see the woman who had occupied his mind repeatedly… and if he played his cards right?

He might secure a second date!

CHAPTER 7

ALICE PULLED UP IN HER VEHICLE ALONG THE CURB AND stared at the house. It was an unassuming house that looked straight out of the seventies. A massive slant to the roof along with octagon windows told her there might be yellow flocked wallpaper or green shag carpet inside.

The rest of the neighborhood didn't look too promising, either. There were cars on blocks, several people were milling around a house further down the street, and everyone seemed to be wearing hooded sweatshirts or baseball caps that nearly covered their eyes. Glancing up at the porch, she saw a little old woman come out and wave.

"And that must be his grandmother," Alice said under her breath, getting out of the car anxiously. She was almost glad that it wasn't Matt, because she might have put the car into gear and run away, as badly as her hands were shaking.

Matt had told her not to bring anything—but Alice wasn't one to show up empty-handed. She had brought a dish of green beans to go with everything else… and now wished she'd brought something a little less ordinary.

… Like a strawberry trifle or a cheesecake…?

But no, no…

She'd brought green beans.

Weeeee. Exciting.

"Hello," Alice called out, smiling anxiously, and walking up to the porch.

"You've got gumption," the older woman said, causing her to freeze immediately in her tracks. Alice nearly chucked the dish over her shoulder and bolted for the car.

"But I like it," she clucked, holding open the door of the house and winking at Alice. "That sassy grandson of mine always gets his way, but us women have to keep him in line, or he will be terrible to deal with. I'm Margie, but you can call me Grams too."

"Are you buttering her up to me?" Matt said from inside the house before appearing.

"Nope. I'm telling her what a brat you truly are—but I love you anyhow, you rascal."

Alice let out her breath and walked shakily the rest of the way up to the door. This was not the greeting she expected, and it was a little nerve-wracking.

"It's very nice to meet you, Margie," Alice said politely. "I brought a side dish."

"I told him you didn't need to bring anything," Margie groused, giving Matt a terse look as he held up his hands innocently.

"I swear, Grams—I told her not to worry about it."

"Did he?" Margie asked pointedly, causing Alice to do a double-take between the two of them. Matt towered over his grandmother by almost a foot and had well over a hundred pounds on the frail, wrinkled woman who was rockin' some blue-tinged curls on her head.

"Yes, he actually said that," Alice began nervously. "… but I didn't feel right coming to eat and not bringing a dish."

"Because you must come from good people," Margie harrumphed. "I bet it's a dessert."

"Why?" Alice blurted out, immediately defensive as the older woman looked her up and down pointedly. "It's actually green beans... and that's a little rude."

"Oh, I do like her. She's a feisty one!" Margie cackled with joy, wrapping her arm around Alice's waist. "C'mon child, let me show you the kitchen. Matt, don't just stand there - make some coffee or something."

Alice looked at Matt, unsure of what exactly was going on and hardly able to believe this little woman was ordering them both about like it was nothing. He just gave a little wave, smiled, and walked past them both towards the kitchen.

This was the craziest greeting she'd ever had... and reminded her a little bit of how Matt dealt with her at the hospital. They both wanted to get their way and didn't give a hoot, so long as it went the way they chose.

Alice was being corralled into the dining area that held a table that was formally set. Plates, folded napkins, utensils, and a flower arrangement were all waiting—reminding her of Thanksgiving at her aunt's house as a young girl.

The room, the house in fact, was actually straight out of the seventies, just like she suspected. Wood paneling adorned the walls. A massive golden fork and spoon about three feet tall were prominently displayed, along with a large oblong lacquered wooden clock, showing the time. A microwave on a metal cart stood in the corner with a log shaped nut tray, complete with two metal tools to crack open the pecans lying in wait.

"Your home is lovely," Alice said nervously, trying to fill in the empty space around them as she was nudged towards a seat at the table.

"Bull hockey," Margie snorted. "But it's my home and I like it."

"Grams is quite set in her ways," Matt began as he entered the dining room, holding two cups of coffee. "I hope you like cream and sugar? The garlic bread isn't quite done yet."

"Still tanning, boy?" Margie asked bluntly, a smile touching her lips.

"You know it," he grinned, winking at his grandmother.

"Okay. I'm super-confused," Alice admitted, looking between the two of them.

"I like my bread a little crispier than my grandmother," Matt explained, setting down one of the brown coffee mugs before her that looked like it had drips of paint in the glaze. "So, I tease her about it being tanned like her favorite actor, Leonardo Di Caprio."

"Ohhh," Alice exclaimed before smiling.

"Now she's got it," Margie grinned. "I bet you are more of a Ryan Reynolds type of girl, aren't you?"

"I do like to laugh," Alice admitted. "But there is something swoon worthy about Captain America."

"Ahhh yes, America's finest keister," the older woman acknowledged, holding up her cup of coffee in mock salute. Alice choked on her sip of coffee, quickly yanking the napkin off the table to cover her mouth.

"I may be old, but I'm certainly not blind."

"I'm practically Captain America on a daily basis, you know?" Matt interjected, taking a seat with his own cup of coffee between the two women at the head of the table.

"Nice try, buster," his grandmother muttered, causing Alice to nearly spray her second sip of coffee. She coughed and laughed, sounding almost squeaky as she struggled to breathe.

"You two should come with a warning," she rasped, grinning at the banter between them.

"Handle with care?" Matt winked.

"Use with extreme caution," Margie warned, making Matt's smile disappear as he got this betrayed look on his face with an adorable pout that had Alice laughing again.

"Contents under pressure?" Alice bantered. "... or better yet—'may cause irritation'."

"Definitely," Matt agreed, sighing happily as he rested his chin on his knuckles, smiling at her. "Smart and beautiful - A perfect combination."

"Knock it off, Casanova," Margie laughed. "I bet the casserole is finished now—if not, it should be before I have to turn down the air-conditioning to keep up with all the hot air spewing in here."

Alice couldn't help the burst of laughter that escaped her.

This had certainly been the most fun introduction she'd had in forever—and the meal promised to be just as lively. She found herself wishing she'd accepted weeks ago as Matt got up, winking at her with this half smirk that was infectious.

It enchanted Alice by how lovely an afternoon she was having. She laughed more today than she had in years, making her side hurt with effort. Matt's grandmother had everyone wrapped around her little gnarled finger just by being spectacularly sassy—and that had obviously rubbed off on her grandson.

Matt was quite charming—and absolutely correct.

He was an incredible cook. It quite surprised Alice to see him shoo-off his grandmother a few times out of the kitchen when he served up their plates instead of bringing out the piping hot casserole dish that sat steaming on top of the gas stove. His grandmother had whispered that the garlic bread that was 'tanning' was actually made from scratch.

"My boy spent the night in the guest room last evening so the dough could rise all night. I'm not a pizza-person, but I suppose it was edible. He made pizza and the rolls trying to impress someone we all know," Margie hissed quietly.

"Hey! I heard that," Matt called out, laughing. "My pizza dough is amazing, and it's all in the throw, ya' know."

"You throw your own dough?" Alice asked in disbelief, because she'd tried it herself a few times and missed catching it quite often. Now she just settled for pounding it out on a cornmeal pan, so it didn't stick.

"I'll have to make pizza for you on our next date…" he invited, wagging his eyebrows.

"Won't be here," Margie interrupted emphatically. "I don't like pizza nor the leftovers."

"Grams, I know you like your spaghetti or lasagna. How about next Sunday, I make you homemade ravioli?"

"No. I prefer the lasagna."

"What do you want?" Matt asked suddenly, his gaze swinging to Alice.

"Oh… I, uh…"

"Alice wants lasagna too," Margie chimed in before she could answer. "And don't cheap out on the cheese. Use the genuine stuff and an egg to bind it together like I taught you. You will be here next Sunday, right?"

Alice blinked at both of them, who sat there looking at her expectantly.

"Pizza on Friday night with me… and then lasagna for Sunday lunch with Grams?" Matt invited softly, staring at her with those big brown eyes that made her toes curl.

"I have to work a late shift on Friday," Alice admitted. "But I'm free on Wednesday evening."

"Me too," Matt confirmed, nodding. "How about I pick you up?"

"Well…" Alice hedged, suddenly nervous, and looked at his grandmother, who was watching the two of them. "How about I bring a nice salad to go with the lasagna on Sunday?"

"Do you cook, girl?"

"Yes. I love cooking."

"How about you come over early, and we'll all make cannolis from scratch for dessert instead?"

"Seriously?" Matt asked, looking at his grandmother in disbelief. "We're gonna make great grandma's Christmas cannolis for dessert? My-my, this *is* an event!"

"Hush boy!" Margie intoned, smiling at Alice. "What do you say?"

"Ricotta or mascarpone cream?" Alice grinned.

"Ricotta, girl… we have Italian in our blood."

"I thought your last name was Jackson? It's not very Italian, you know."

"Only because of some silly romantic lovesick fool long ago in our family tree," Margie acknowledged, waving, and smiling softly. "Remind you of anyone we know?"

Matt actually had the good grace to flush and rub the back of his neck nervously, looking away. Alice was a little surprised to see him quiet for once and at a loss for words. She was also surprised that his grandmother hinted he might actually truly like her.

"Sounds like I have my plans for the week," she found herself saying easily, as Matt's eyes slid towards her again, dancing with joy and something more that made her stomach flip pleasantly in her midsection.

As the afternoon wrapped up, Margie insisted on walking the yard together while Matt cleaned up. She showed her all of her flowers, her vegetable garden, and told her stories about Matt as a child. It was a little surprising at how open the woman was towards her… talking like they were old friends. Barbie was running around the yard, barking at everything that moved.

Not a single bug was safe from the large animal, Alice mused, smiling at the dog, as she flopped down on top of something and began rolling wildly in the grass.

This was probably the most pleasant day she'd had in forever, and it gave Alice such a burst of happiness knowing that they had already invited her back to join them.

"I really must be getting home," she announced regretfully, patting Margie's hand where the older woman had taken her arm to steady her gait about the yard.

"I know—and I am very glad you came today."

"I appreciate the invitation."

"That's all Matt," Margie smiled, "... and my boy has excellent taste."

"We are just friends."

"Of course you are."

Matt slid open the back door of the house and leaned against the frame, drying his hands on a towel from the kitchen.

"How's my three favorite girls?" he called out playfully.

"Two out of the three need to go to the bathroom," Margie announced baldly, causing Alice to burst out laughing at the outrageous woman beside her.

"I'm guessing the other is Barbie?" Matt chuckled.

"He's clever and nice to look at," Margie teased, releasing Alice's arm and making her way towards the house. Matt immediately took a spot at her side, helping her make her way up the steps to the back door before she disappeared inside.

He turned to look at Alice.

"It's nice to see you smiling so much," Matt began.

"She's a hoot," Alice admitted. "It makes it easy."

"Now you understand that being a smart-aleck is all in the genes," he teased, smiling at her. "I can't seem to help myself nor control what comes flying out of my mouth."

"Maybe you need a warning label," Alice sassed, remembering the conversation earlier in the afternoon.

"Ohhh maybe? And what would that warning label be, angel? Maybe something spicy, like 'caution—contents hot'...?" he asked suggestively, taking a step closer to her.

Alice chuckled, shaking her head.

"How about 'caution—may be harmful'?"

"Nahhh..." Matt breathed, smiling as he took her hand in his.

The feeling of his rough fingers against her own skin gave her goosebumps. He was incredibly attractive, but it was that charming personality that kept her on her toes that made him so very fascinating. She adored a guy who could make her smile, and he seemed to have no issues with that.

"How about...," Matt continued on, taking her other hand in his. "'Could cause feelings of warmth'?"

"Oh ho! You certainly think highly of yourself, don't you?" she laughed at his clever wit... but her laugh faltered as he took a step closer to her. Her heart pounded in her chest as she realized he was close enough to see the scruff on his chin and a faint scar on his cheek.

"Maybe my warning should be a little more scandalous," he breathed softly, leaning down towards her. Alice found herself leaning towards him of her own accord, curious and a little frightened of what kissing him would be like.

"Like what?" she whispered, unable to help herself.

"Do not put in mouth..." he breathed, hovering just over her lips. "But that would stop this from happening between us, wouldn't it? And neither of us wants that to happen."

"What *is* this...?" Alice hesitated, her voice the barest whisper and full of emotion.

"Great question!" Margie hollered, causing Alice to step back immediately, releasing Matt's hands. He tried to cling to her hand for a moment longer, but she pulled away regardless, hurrying to the door as if seeking shelter from an oncoming storm of certain emotional turmoil.

"Grams…" he said with a heavy sigh, running his hand through is hair in frustration.

"Don't you 'Grams' me, boy," Margie said, shaking her finger at him. "I told you to take your time, Casanova, and schmoozing the girl like that was *not* going slow—even if it was a clever line. You get that from your grandpa. I'll give you that much…"

"I've got to go," Alice said quickly, taking the chance for escape so she could gather her thoughts. "Thank you for everything."

"We'll see you next Sunday," Margie announced as a reminder.

"Wednesday," Matt corrected quickly.

"I'll text you."

Alice didn't stick around to see what either of them said. Instead, she grabbed her purse and practically ran from the house—and from Matt. He was so intense and came on so very strongly that she wasn't prepared for it. He was going to kiss her, and she had stood there like a deer in headlights, just waiting for it to happen!

She hopped into her car, ignored everything going on around her, and quickly drove off. Her phone beeped from inside her purse and right now her hands were shaking so badly that she couldn't imagine reading it. If she tried, she would probably wreck her car.

She already knew it was probably Matt texting her and he would just have to wait.

CHAPTER 8

ALICE TRIED NOT TO PANIC OR BACK OUT OF THEIR DATE tonight due to nerves. What if he regretted it or changed his mind? Today was Wednesday. She'd tried to play it cool the last two days—and had succeeded until last night.

Bless his heart, Matt was trying to give her space.

He had only contacted her once to ask if she liked pepperoni and mushrooms on her pizza. They hadn't established a time, whether she was having him pick her up, if she should bring something to accompany the pizza... or anything at all!

He was just giving her the space she'd asked for—and she was hating it more and more with each passing moment. She'd never imagined herself as clingy or needy, but she found herself trying to find stuff that amused her or kept her mind occupied. She missed laughing, and Sunday had been full of laughter.

The comfort her animals gave her at home, their superbly snuggable furry coats and floofy tails helped, but only a little bit. She missed that brief warm touch of Matt's hand and the way it jolted her system. The way he watched her... she missed that most of all.

He was intense—there was no doubt! But that singular look he would give her, the unabashed admiration when he thought she wasn't looking... that stayed with Alice.

It haunted her.

She realized that no one ever looked at her like that, nor were they ever just that open of a personality. His eyes hid no secrets when he looked at her... and maybe that was what made her so nervous. There were no secrets, no hidden agendas to figure out, and no playful dating games.

He was interested in her... period.

Alice was standing at the nurses' station, lost in thought, when she heard a slow whistle of appreciation come from one of the ladies nearby. As if the world was moving in slow motion, Alice raised her eyes from the chart to see Matt heading this way... in a dead-sexy swagger that could turn asphalt back into a liquid state.

He was sauntering down the hallway of the hospital in his police uniform. He was dressed head-to-toe in black, with some dark sunglasses on. Even the scruff on his chin was creating a deep shadow against his beautiful, tanned skin.

His holster was slung over his shoulders, making them appear just that much larger, while his thumb was hooked onto his belt. The other hand was playfully slinging a set of handcuffs around in a spinning motion that was absolutely and utterly suggestive to no end...

"MmmmmMmm!" Lola grunted emphatically. "Lord have mercy on my soul, because I'm about to commit a felony right here, right now! Mmm yes, child! Do you see the swagger on that fine man headed this way?"

"Lola!" Alice hissed.

"What? I ain't sayin' nuthin' that y'all weren't thinking!"

she retorted, high-fiving another nurse nearby, who had been the one that whistled aloud.

Matt walked slowly, as if he knew he looked incredibly good in his uniform and was putting on a show... but for who? Her? The other nurses? Was he trying to embarrass her, because if so, he was succeeding incredibly well!

"Mmmph!" Lola grunted again, unabashedly waving. "Right here, officer! I'm ready to go! Whatever it was—I confess! I did it!"

"Oh my word, just kill me now," Alice groaned, putting her head down into her hands as she leaned heavily on the nurses' station.

This could not get any worse at all, could it?

Someone grabbed her arm, pulling it out from under her head, nearly causing her to face plant into the counter, but she caught herself at the last moment... when she heard the clink of metal and felt it encircle her wrist.

A surge of laughter filled the room as she stared in horror at the cuff, then up into Matt's grinning face. He held up the other cuff and promptly clicked it on his own wrist.

Whistles and catcalls echoed in the hallway as he began dragging her away from the nurse's station.

"What? Wait a second... WAIT!" Alice hollered, tugging on her wrist painfully. "You can't just come in here, and..."

"Yep," Matt interrupted. "I can—and I did."

"No. You can't," she argued. "It's called 'abuse of power', you nincompoop."

"You are under arrest," he said in a low voice, looking around. He whipped off his sunglasses and tucked them into his shirt pocket like it was just another day at the job.

"For *what*?" she balked.

"Stealing my heart?" he suggested, smiling tenderly at her.

Alice felt her mouth drop open as a chorus of 'awwwws' filled the air. She stared up at him for a few moments and shook her head in disbelief. He was the most outrageous man that seemed to have literally no filter when it came to his mouth.

Matt shrugged.

... And scooped her up, depositing her over his shoulder!

Her arm was pinned painfully on her back, nearly on her bottom, as his own arm rested nearby—still tethered to hers. He was hauling her off like she was nothing... and that meant everything to her.

Growing up, she'd always been one of the tallest girls in her class. She hated gym class because of her weight and curvy shape. There were all sorts of descriptions used by teachers, nurses, doctors, or counselors meant to make her feel better.

Healthy.

Statuesque.

Well-built.

Shapely.

Curvy.

A handful.

... But never, in her entire life, had she felt *delicate* —until now.

The fact that he hauled her up over his shoulder like she was nothing had left her reeling. It was that display of strength, the sheer masculinity and rugged caveman attitude he was showing that took her breath away, keeping her from struggling or fighting this moment.

"Ladies? My girl is going home sick..." he announced, turning, and walking down the hallway towards the exit. As they exited the building and came up to the squad car, she heard him finally speak.

"Be careful, angel. When I let you down, take it easy, so neither of us has to go right back inside," Matt cautioned apologetically. "I was so taken aback by your gorgeous appearance that I didn't think things through and I'm sorry for that."

"For what?"

"Because one of us might wrench an arm when I put you down."

"Because of my weight?" she squawked angrily, seeing red immediately.

"What? NO!" he balked, looking shocked and appalled. "Because I thought it would be cute to handcuff you and whisk you away, but I didn't think it would hurt quite so much."

"Oh," Alice said, deflating almost immediately. "Are you okay?"

"No?" he chuckled. "But I'm loving the view."

"You wretch!" she squeaked, slapping at his back, before she started laughing herself.

"What's so funny?"

"Truthfully?" Alice admitted, feeling her face flush with embarrassment. "I am too. Definitely Captain America's keister…"

Matt burst out laughing, raising his other hand up to hold her in place so that way she didn't fall—injuring them both. She didn't want to focus on where his hand was placed right now, only the fact that they were both laughing at the absurdity of the situation.

It was terribly uncomfortable… and so very romantic in the weirdest way.

Just like him.

Alice smiled and poked him on the lower spine.

"How about you try leaning us both onto the trunk of the car and we manage to untwist ourselves somehow without tearing a tendon or breaking something out of socket?"

"My brilliant girl," he announced, patting her directly on the bottom, causing her to jolt in alarm.

"Hey! Stop that!"

"Yes ma'am," he chuckled.

They leaned slowly over the trunk and Matt carefully unwound his arm, moving slowly with Alice so they could get untangled. He only cursed once... or three times, whereas she managed to move almost unimpeded. As she sat up, she saw that he was taking most of the abuse from the cuffs, leaving her unmarked.

His wrist was pretty mangled, turning various shades of red and purple where it was still tethered to hers. There were even spots where the skin had sloughed off, leaving shiny spots.

He was trying to put the key in the tiny hole and nearly dropped it.

"Here," Alice offered, taking the key. She easily inserted it in the cuff and then hesitated, looking up into his dark eyes.

Neither of them moved.

This was the craziest thing to be happening to her.

Alice was sitting on a cop car in the hospital parking lot, handcuffed to the most incredible guy she'd ever had the fortune to meet... and she was a fool to let this moment slip by.

She'd wanted happy memories like in the movies—and this could certainly be one of them if she would only meet Matt halfway.

Without unlocking the handcuffs, Alice released the key, leaving it dangling in the slot between their hands. Instead, she reached up and cupped his neck, encouraging him silently to finish the movement that she had started.

"Are you sure?" he asked, hesitating, his eyes watching hers.

A sting of tears touched her eyes—because here he was, being thoughtful and giving her the chance to back away again.

64

She touched his cheek, feeling the rough stubble, before letting her thumb brush against his lips. His dark eyes resembled melted chocolate at the warm surge of emotion within them.

"Let's just say that I feel safe right now," Alice admitted softly, pointing at the cuffs.

He chuckled softly, closing the gap between them.

Matt pressed his lips to hers, and the world stopped spinning. Everything faded away as every sense within her suddenly focused on that single, simple icon of affection. He tasted like coffee and joy rolled into one—leaving her craving more.

As quickly as he'd kissed her, it was over.

"I could do that for hours," he whispered softly, gently caressing his nose against hers. "But for our first kiss, it's not bad…"

"Excuse me?" Alice blurted out, straightening up and looking at him in shock.

"I'm teasing," he admitted, smiling. "But I really need to get this handcuff off and put some peroxide on it. It's going to leave a pretty wicked mark on my wrist. I'm lucky there's still skin on my wrist bone."

"You, big baby!" Alice retorted, inserting the key and laughing in disbelief. "Here I thought you were some big macho tough guy that could handle anything…"

"And I am," he asserted quickly, slipping the cuffs back into his belt holster. Taking her by the waist, he picked her up off the back of the squad car and set her down on the ground gently.

"Well, for not grunting or complaining about my weight? I guess I could treat it while you…"

"Oh halleluiah—are we playing doctor?"

The sheer enthusiasm combined with the scandalous

suggestion made Alice throw back her head and laugh out loud at his unbridled excitement.

"Stop it," she chuckled. "Can't you be serious for once?"

"Never," he smiled, leaning down to kiss her quickly. "I adore your laugh and want to hear it as much as possible."

He held out his hand, palm up, and waited beside her.

"I can follow you in my car," Alice hesitated, smiling shyly.

"Or you could let me do the whole 'boyfriend-thing' and allow me to whisk you away to my place? I promise only to 'wine-and-dine' you—but I will never say 'no' to another kiss should you decide you can't resist my roguish charms another moment longer…"

Matt winked at her playfully with a slightly upturned smile—but it was the momentary hesitation and the look in his eyes that caught her attention.

He was concerned that *she* would reject *him*…

Alice moved to put her hand in his—and hesitated. She looked him in the eyes and saw the indecision warring in his.

"I'll have you know that I'm an extremely boring person," she began nervously. "… And insecure to a fault. So, this is a little scary for me. I've never had anyone look at me like you do."

"I'm full of hot air and make a lot of dumb comments," Matt admitted, his eyes raking hers. "But I believe in being yourself and who cares what anyone else thinks."

"I care."

"I know—and that is why I'm standing here waiting," he admitted. Their hands weren't touching yet, but he wouldn't move to grasp hers either.

"I think you are gorgeous, incredibly smart, and there is something about you that just makes my brain melt into my shoes. So, if that's boring…?" Matt hesitated before smiling tenderly at her.

"Yeah. I dig 'boring' and it's my most favorite thing, ever."

The sheer honesty in his gaze made her catch her breath.

"I'm trusting you," she whispered softly, placing her hand in his and reveling in the feel of his warm palm.

"I know you are, angel," he breathed, pulling her hand up to his lips and kissing the back of it. "I will never let you down. Now, do you like stuffed crust, 'cause I bought some fresh mozzarella…"

Alice laughed again as he changed subject mid-conversation like it was nothing and began walking her over to the passenger door of the cruiser.

"Now, no playing with the computer or googling yourself on there. This is serious stuff. In fact, no touching anything in the car… unless it's me."

Matt winked, shutting the door.

HOURS LATER, Alice was in sheer heaven.

She had been nervous about this evening, but the humble sincerity in everything Matt said or did was quite refreshing. If he said he was hungry, he was… there were no guessing games.

Matt was the biggest, whiniest baby when it came to her doctoring his wrist—reminding her of his time in the hospital and how they'd met. He was nearly that demanding then, too.

He actually got teary-eyed and winced when she put peroxide on it and some triple antibiotic ointment before bandaging it. This big ol' hulking guy could rip off his tape but whined at how 'the peroxide stung' his wrist.

But they were two peas in a pod as well…

Matt's house had a massive kitchen that he'd worked on over the last several years, she found out. He'd knocked down a wall in the house, gutted the cabinets, and started over from scratch, turning it into the kitchen of anyone's dreams.

When he said he liked to cook... Matt had meant it!

There were drawers full of tools for everything that anyone could ever ask for. Whisks of different sizes, some silicone and some metal. Wooden spoons, slotted stainless spoons, and nonstick pasta spoons. Knives of all shapes and sizes were placed in a drawer that had a specific spot for each of them.

Alice thought she liked to cook—but this guy was a do-it-yourself chef!

He showed her his favorite tomato knife and had her slice the Roma tomatoes that were ripened on the counter. She watched in awe as he began tossing the blob of dough into an actual crust, just as he'd bragged that he could. They stood there together, slicing up vegetables and building the pizza, before sliding it into the gas oven.

Matt poured each of them a glass of wine and then looked around sheepishly. Gone was the confident, suave man...

"What's wrong?" she asked, smiling.

"I just realized that I spend most of my time cooking or working... that I don't have a nice table setting like Grams does."

"Where do you normally eat your dinner?" she asked, realizing that he was right. There was no kitchen table or dining room table to be seen.

"Truthfully?" Matt winced. "I usually end up eating on a TV tray on the couch or wolfing my food down 'cause I lost track of time and need to head out."

"TV trays sound ideal then—or do you have a table outside on the patio? I don't suppose you watch anything I would like, do you?"

He let out a shaky sigh and visibly shivered.

"Let's not even talk about the backyard right now. That is next year's project for the house. I'd like to put a wood-burning pizza oven back there, and a deck."

"That's sounds lovely."

"Maybe you can help me plan it," he said quietly, watching her.

"You sure move fast, don't you?" she replied bluntly, feeling a flutter of nervousness in her stomach.

"Maybe?" he admitted, before smiling at her. "Or maybe you just need a little more time. One of these days, you are going to be so thrilled to see me that you are going to finally let all those walls down and just admit that you are crazy about me."

"Or that I'm just crazy…" she teased nervously.

"Or that too," he grinned, holding up his wineglass to her. "To being crazy together…"

"You know, I like that…" she admitted. "To being crazy together."

They both took a sip of the wine, and Alice savored the heady flavors of the sweet red fluid as it touched her tongue. She never really partook of alcohol much, but when he'd popped the cork? She was tossing caution to the wind and trying to relax—this would only help!

"I'm so glad I met you," Matt said quietly, standing there leaning on the counter and staring at his glass of wine. "I wish it was under better circumstances, but I don't think I would have changed much… except for the near fatal head wound."

He smiled at her softly before looking back at his wine-glass, swirling the red liquid around.

"That's so sweet of you," Alice whispered, unsure what to say to that because it was so candid and so unexpected.

"I know it's crazy—and that seems to be a theme lately," he teased before growing somber. "But I would go flying through the air again, take a bullet, or get in a car wreck, if it meant waking up and seeing that beautiful smile for the first time, all over again. I can't explain how special that moment was, but it was magical."

There was such longing, such wonder in his voice, that she couldn't help but feel a surge of emotion within her. It was like a flower unfurling within her chest and filling every space within her with this incredible longing to make him smile again.

"Maybe it was the drugs?" she said sheepishly, realizing that it would be so easy to fall for this man before her.

Matt burst out laughing, setting down his wineglass. He pulled her unabashedly into his arms, hugging her, and continued to chuckle lightly. Alice just stood there, in the circle of his embrace, as it hit her. She quickly realized that maybe it didn't have to be all fireworks, rainbows, and unicorns...

Maybe falling in love started with just an unexpected hug and a smile?

CHAPTER 9

ALICE HATED WORKING THIRD SHIFT AT THE HOSPITAL. ALL THE car wrecks, the crazy people, and the overdose victims seemed to come in on a Saturday night—especially when it coincided with a full moon.

Tonight was no different.

Every bed was full in the unit and every story spectacular. She had an accidental overdose on a person who'd never used drugs before that was coming down off the effects, currently sedated in one of the rooms. Another room held a man who was trying to lose weight by starving himself, guzzling water, and dosing repeatedly on laxatives. One of the other beds had a woman who insisted she swallowed a spider, and it was trying to crawl back up her throat.

Alice shivered.

That particular one gave her the 'willies'…

The last patient seemed to be almost too normal.

He was a quiet, middle-aged man, father of four, with abdominal pain. So far, all the labs had come back fine, and she was waiting to hear from the doctor on duty because she truthfully wasn't sure why he was still admitted. The man had no fever, no delusional rantings, nothing... just said that he had a pain in his abdomen.

Matt had texted earlier that he was on duty, offering Starbucks and a shoulder to snooze on when she got off work at seven in the morning. That was one thing about him—he kept her smiling constantly.

Code Silver in the ER!
I repeat, Code Silver in the ER!

Alice blinked, looking up at the speaker mounted in the ceiling of creepy-spider-lady's room in shock and disbelief. Feeling ashamed, she realized that she'd tuned out the woman's rantings, but now heard the commotion just outside the room. There was a flurry of voices, and she knew why now.

A Code Silver meant there was a threat or an active shooter present... and she was in the ER with them.

"I can feel it again..." the old woman screeched, pulling at the skin on her neck. "He's moving and trying to get away!"

Alice immediately tossed the chart onto the bed, running over to her side and trying to shush the lady physically. The woman's hands fought her, slapping at her, but she couldn't allow her to keep scratching at her neck, nor did she want any undue attention from whatever was going on out in the hallway to come in here! The woman was leaving red gouges in her skin—but it would be nothing compared to what a bullet could do, and let's face it.

There was absolutely no way a spider was in her throat trying to crawl out—but getting shot was now a genuine possibility.

"Shhh! Please," Alice whispered, feeling suddenly sick. "Something's wrong."

"The spider! She's moving!"

"Shhh! I know. I know… we are going to get someone to help you, but you have to be really quiet, so the spider doesn't know we are going to get rid of it."

The woman's eyes went round as saucers.

"Oh, good idea…" she breathed, holding up her finger to her lips.

Whew… Alice thought to herself, listening for any definitive sounds outside the door. She could hear voices yelling but it was all muffled, and she could not distinguish whether it was her coworkers or someone else.

Slipping her phone from her scrub top, she immediately texted Matt… praying he didn't call, giving her away.

Something's wrong at work.
I'm calling 911 now—just know I'm safe… I think.
My phone is on silent

Alice felt tears burning as she realized she wanted to say so much more—and didn't feel like she should. Things could be alright. This could be a mistake that was quickly remedied… or so she hoped.

Dialing emergency, she slipped into the bathroom to speak. Before she shut the door, she held up her fingers to her lips, looking back at the patient lying in the bed watching her.

"I'm going to call someone to get the spider," Alice fibbed, hating the way her voice shook. "I'm going to step away, so the spider doesn't hear me."

"Thank you."

"Shhh, we have to be quiet."

The woman nodded, looking so hopeful and cheery that it broke Alice's heart as she said several prayers as the door slid shut.

"Hello?" Alice whispered in a hushed breath as soon as a voice answered. "I can't speak long, but I'm a nurse and something's wrong. They've called for an active shooter, and I can hear yelling."

"Where are you?"

"With a patient in one of the rooms in the ER."

"Are you safe?"

"Yes, but I can't latch the door—and I can't block it without making noises or calling attention to us. I'm hiding in the bathroom trying not to be heard right now."

"Your patient—are they injured?"

"I don't think so," Alice admitted. "We are still waiting on labs and the doctor's orders. I was here taking her vitals and…"

"Stay put."

Alice blinked at the curt order that made a chill run down her spine. She listened as someone was talking in the background.

"Miss?"

"Yes. I'm here."

"Someone else called it in, too—you are in danger. There is an active shooter in the building and police are on the way. I need you to stay calm and get your patient. Can you move them?"

"Maybe? I think so."

"Whatever you do—stay in that room. Alright? And don't hang up the phone. We are here to help you."

"I'm not hanging up."

"Good. Now, can you go get your patient and lock both of you in the bathroom?"

An alarm suddenly started chiming, and she recognized the buzzer. It was from the bed remote, and someone was calling for assistance. A shiver of dread ran down her spine as she knew deep down inside exactly who'd pressed the call button... because if Alice had any luck?

It was bad luck.

"Oh, no..." she breathed, cracking open the bathroom door to see the woman on the bed waving happily and pointing at the remote.

"I'm tired of waiting—so I called an exterminator," the patient called out happily.

"Oh, I sincerely hope not..." Alice whispered painfully at the morbid, unintended pun. "I've gotta go. The call button got pressed and I'm out of time. Please send someone quick. Emergency room three-twelve..."

Alice pressed disconnect and dropped her phone back into her pocket without checking her messages as the hospital room door burst open before her very eyes.

MATT WAS SCARFING down a burger and feeding bits of it to Barbie as they waited in their cruiser, listening to the radio. The feed was pretty active tonight and a full moon brought out the lunatics. He'd already had to work three accidents, one flasher, and was currently finishing up paperwork on a speeding ticket.

He hated night shifts.

It almost caused him to reschedule lunch with his grand-mother and Alice simply, so he could get a little rest... or give him a chance to gather himself so he was in a better mood. It had been a long night and the only thing he had to look forward to was seeing Alice in a few hours... despite the fatigue. He was planning on bringing her coffee and hoped she was truly tempted to use his shoulder for a pillow.

It wasn't romantic in the slightest—but sometimes life just didn't allow it. To him, it was better that Alice see the worst of him so she understood he's just a flawed person like anyone else.

Problem was, she was utterly perfect in his book.

"Barbie… she's gonna think I'm nuts," he crooned to his dog, tearing off a bit of hamburger. "I swear I'm crazy about that woman."

The German Shepherd angled her head sideways as if she understood and began wagging her tail. Matt took a big sip of his soda and put away his things.

"We've gotta get back to it, sweet girl," he told the dog, who barked happily.

Matt ruffled the dog's ears and ignored it when she snapped at him playfully. Barbie had the same personality he did, and they just seemed to get along. He could have never imagined how much he would grow to love this dog two years ago when he graduated from the Academy.

That had been such a magical time—such an honor!

He'd been accepted into the K-9 specialty unit of Disaster City Search and Rescue located just outside of Dallas. It had been a dream come true and something he never imagined would happen. He was a kid from the streets, growing up in a rough part of town, and had nearly been raised from the age of thirteen by his grandmother.

It was part of the reason he joined—and part of the reason he was so protective of his Grams. His parents had been killed in a drunk driving accident on one New Year's Eve, turning his life upside down.

His father had been a Dallas Police Sergeant and Matt knew that someone had recommended him in memory of his father. Being part of the force meant they accepted you in their 'family'… his name was known. They had accepted him into their flock immediately after graduation from the police academy.

But the nomination?

No, he hadn't expected that and would be forever grateful.

It was humbling, and he would never let his mysterious benefactor down. Picking up the radio, he started up his vehicle and backed out of the parking spot.

"10-98" Matt said easily in the mic, announcing he was resuming patrol and available for the next call if needed.

"10-06 Standby," crackled on the radio.

That was surprising. The radio chatter ceased almost immediately. The dispatcher only used that code in severe emergencies. Hitting the brakes, he was glad he hadn't pulled out onto the road yet, because when they said 'standby'... they meant 'wait for orders'.

Something was up.

"I've got a 10-39 in progress at University Medical Center. I repeat, 10-39 in progress. 10-45 all units. Active shooter reported."

"10-04 copy... on route to University Trauma Medical Center," Matt announced, feeling his blood run cold as his burger sat like a lump in his stomach. He'd been to University a few times recently—once when he was injured and the other time to sweep Alice off her feet, literally.

Picking up his cell phone, he groaned aloud as he realized that he'd accidentally hit the volume button while it was in his pocket, effectively putting the thing on silent.

He saw the brief text message and swallowed back bile.

Something's wrong at work.
I'm calling 911 now—just know I'm safe... I think.
My phone is on silent

The words were glaringly bright on the tiny screen.

Matt knew Alice was there working—but seeing her text made him realize that his sweet, sunshine-y angel was in the middle of a wretched nightmare and could possibly become a statistic before his very eyes.

He wanted to tell her so many things. The words, the emotions behind it, and the raw turbulence within him were screaming the fragmented sentences aloud in his head... yet silence surrounded him.

I'm on my way...
Don't be scared...
I'll save you or die trying...
I love you...

Letting out a ragged breath, he uttered a soulful prayer that she was alright. Her phone actually was on silent. He wanted to text her, to let her know he'd received her message and to be brave... but he couldn't risk it. Instead, he would have to remain silent for her sake—and his.

"Focus, Jackson," he breathed, drawing in a deep breath and trying to find some peace of mind within him somewhere. He needed to keep his thoughts straight, his focus sharp, and remove any emotion from what was about to occur around him.

Nervously, he radioed in again, trying to find a routine—something that felt normal.

"Officer on route to University Medical Center," he repeated and shook his head. "Barbie? We've gotta go help our girl..."

Barbie let out a massive bark right behind his ear, causing him to flinch as he pulled into the street, tires squealing. Matt flipped on the lights and sirens, mashing the accelerator down to the floor. The engine revved as the world around him turned into a massive blur of lights with one singular focus in mind.

Alice.

THE DOOR to the hospital room burst open in a flurry and the quiet, middle-aged father of four was standing there, covered in blood. He had a revolver in his hand and the calm demeanor was gone—replaced with a distant, detached, haunted look in his eyes that Alice knew would give her nightmares forever.

It was one thing to see a drugged patient halfway between conscious and unconscious... it was completely another to see someone lingering between sane and insane.

He stared blankly, surveying the room, and holding the gun upwards as if he was struggling to hold it.

"Did you come to get the spider?" the woman in the bed asked bluntly.

"No," he said simply, angling his head as if he was listening to something. Alice had a horrible realization that both of them were heavily drugged and not in their right minds. She had thought him calm earlier, but that was only because he was either high when she checked him or he'd gotten a hold of something in the meantime to cause this episode.

His dark eyes looked almost soulless as the pupils were extremely large because of the dilation... but he wasn't wincing at the lights in the hospital room. Clearly, he was pretty far 'out there' right now and that meant 'dangerous'.

"Can I help you?" Alice whispered softly in what she hoped was her least threatening voice possible. He turned towards her, and his dull gaze suddenly sharpened.

"I've been telling you all night that my stomach hurts, but you aren't listening to me. It hurts here," he said angrily, slapping repeatedly at his upper abdomen. "Here! Here! Here!"

"I understand..."

"Since *when?*" he snarled. "Now that I've got your attention?"

"You've always had my attention."

"No, I haven't. You are in here with this crazy lady…"

"Hey!" the woman from the bed interjected, struggling to sit up.

"… And she won't shut up about a spider when I am actually sick," he barked. "I'm sick and no one will help me."

"I'll help you," Alice offered, holding up her hands in a non-threatening manner. "I would be happy to help you, just tell me what you need."

"I need something to make the pain go away—and I need some fool doctor to help me."

"I can help you—but we don't want to hurt anyone in the process, do we?"

"No. I just want it to stop," he said brokenly. Alice saw the blood was dripping from somewhere under his hospital gown and realized that he was indeed having some sort of issue.

"You're bleeding. Let me help you," she began, taking a step forward towards him. He jerked the gun upwards, no longer wobbly or shaking, and held it firm with his finger on the trigger.

Alice froze.

"I want something for the pain," he growled through clenched teeth. "Not another test, not another doctor, and certainly not another lie…"

"You're right," Alice acknowledged softly. "Let me take you down to the pharmacy and let's get you something strong to take away the pain."

"Are you going to kill me?" he asked tautly.

"I could ask you the same question…"

Her voice trembled as she stood there with her hands in the air. He seemed to hesitate and got this distant look on his face again. Part of her thought about jumping for the gun, but with his finger still on the trigger—she didn't dare. Instead, she pointed at the door.

"The pharmacy is on this floor and not too far away. Can we walk there slowly together?" Alice offered, holding out her hand. Maybe if he could trust her, believed she would help him, then she could get him to lower the firearm.

"You go first," he said weakly, pointing at the door with the gun. "You go out there first and tell them to get away from me."

"Sure thing."

Alice slowly made her way to the door and gingerly opened it—half afraid that someone would think that she was the gunman. She certainly didn't want to get shot in the back—but neither did she want to get injured by some unforeseen hero.

Instead, she opened the door slowly and stuck out her hand, palm splayed open.

"We are coming out and everyone needs to clear the hallway," Alice called out. "Please empty the room—now!"

"Alice-hon," one of the nurses called out. "Are you okay, honey?"

"I'm fine," she replied quickly. "Get the hall clear fast. We are going to the pharmacy, and I need to make sure no one is in our way."

"You got it."

Alice stood still for several minutes as she listened to her team yell at everyone to clear the area. You could hear movement, hear footsteps, and she wondered how many people were out there in the waiting area that had to be herded away.

"We are coming out..." she warned softly, not looking back to see if the man was still behind her. She already knew he was because she could smell the sharp, tangy, metallic scent of blood. If she was lucky, he'd faint from blood loss, and she could run for help.

If she was unlucky...

Well... she didn't want to think about that.

Stepping into the hallway, she saw faint flashes in the distance from the parking lot and saw it was police cars. Her breath hitched in her throat as she realized that if he saw the officers, he might panic.

"Alright," she said gently, holding up her hands still. "The way is clear, and we'll have you feeling better in no time."

"You better."

"I will. I promise."

"Maybe I should make you want some pain medicine too?" he said slowly, causing Alice to freeze in her tracks there in the middle of the hallway.

"Sir," Alice began weakly, feeling sick to her stomach. "I really don't want you to shoot me, and I only want to help you. If you hurt me, then I can't get you the pain medicine because it will slow me down."

"Good point."

"We'll be there any moment - just follow me."

Alice walked up to the pharmacy window and rang the buzzer, praying someone hadn't alerted them. Her badge and employee number weren't programmed to get her into the locked pharmacy—only the pharmacy staff could enter the area.

Nurses always buzzed in for assistance or had the medication tubed to their location in the building if they were on another floor. In the ER, they had carts brought around by staff... and in urgent cases?

A pharmacist could be called onto the floor to deliver medication. She hated doing that because it delayed prescriptions for others who might be in dire need.

Just like her—right now.

"Hello?" Alice said desperately, mashing on the buzzer and banging on the glass. "I need some Fentanyl please—it's urgent. Hello? Hello?"

"I thought you said you could help me? Open the door!"

"I'm trying to get someone…" Alice whimpered, flinching, and expecting to get shot at any moment. Her mind was racing with all sorts of fragmented thoughts. She was afraid for her very life and realizing that she had missed out on so much.

This couldn't be happening.

She was supposed to have brunch with Matt and his grandmother tomorrow. They were going to make cannolis and… and she wanted to see his smile again, just one more time.

"OPEN THE DOOR!" he screamed at her, spittle flying. "OPEN THE DOOR! OPENTHEDOOROPENITOPENIT…"

"I'm trying!" she sobbed, banging on the glass even harder. "I know you are in there hiding. Please, please, please just slide a tablet of Fentanyl onto the counter to where I can reach it."

"I can't," came the faintest feminine whisper from somewhere nearby. "I'm only a tech and I don't have a key. It's in the narcotics vault."

Alice turned slowly, her whole body tight with coiled horror as she saw something move in the corner of her peripheral vision. The gun was swinging upwards in an arc towards the doorway.

Everything was moving in slow-motion.

She saw the puff of smoke from the barrel and heard the pop, immediately sending her hands over her ears at the reverberation of sound that made her teeth shake as she pinched her eyes closed tightly.

The handle on the pharmacy door exploded, sending bits of metal flying in all directions as it curled from the impact of the bullet. Another pop had Alice ducking out of the way, back behind the small row of chairs.

"ALICE!"

She recognized that voice and opened her eyes to see Matt's concerned and horrified expression. She could see several officers were moving stealthily within the building, ducked down behind counters or walls nearby... but not Matt.

He stood there bravely, against all odds, with Barbie at his side.

The massive dog looked like she was about to lose her ever-lovin' mind. The sides of her mouth were curled, baring those fearsome canines that had earned her the nickname Cujo by some of the nurses. Foam spittle was dripping onto the floor and Alice could now hear the deep-seated rumbling growls from within the dog's chest.

She never wanted to be on that animal's bad side!

Matt reached for his gun, swinging his arm upwards at the same time that her captor turned towards him. If Alice thought everything was in slow motion before, things just got exponentially slower...

She watched as Matt released the leash, the nylon strap collapsing on itself onto the floor as the dog's muzzle snapped open and shut repeatedly. She knew she should hear the barking, but her mind was slowly blocking out this nightmare, so her brain didn't short out with such a mental overload.

As Matt's arm swung upwards, Alice watched as the man's blood-covered arm tightened perceptibly.

He was going to shoot!

She launched from her position towards him, seeing Matt's eyes widen perceptibly as he saw he was about to get shot. Several other officers drew their guns—and Alice realized she was putting herself directly in the line of fire.

If they shot at the man, she was going to get it.

If she didn't stop him, then Matt was going be injured or worse.

Matt's mouth opened and Alice expected him to holler 'no'... but instead, as she contacted the patient's arm—she heard the strangest thing and was sure her mind was not functioning right.

In a terse voice she'd never heard before, Matt hollered a single word in another language.

"**FASS!**"

Barbie shot off the ground from her spot like some horrific monster. Alice barely got out of the way of the dog as the animal's entire jaw clamped down on the patient's arm, causing him to wail in pain and fear. Several of Barbie's paws contacted Alice, scratching her unmercifully through her clothing, scrambling to get traction to take down this assailant.

The dog bit and bit at the man, repeatedly.

Barbie's muzzle latched on, shaking him bodily as the gun clattered to the floor, causing Alice to flinch as it fired. A mist of white smoke crept from the wall where the bullet hit as scream after scream echoed in the hallway.

She couldn't pull her eyes away from Barbie... or the patient.

Strong, warm hands clamped down on her painfully, yanking her bodily away from the scene as the dog thrashed the man around.

Alice was in shock, and she knew it. She was trembling and could hardly move.

Matt walked past her, putting himself between her and the man who'd held her captive. Several other officers surrounded the animal who was subduing the man and Alice was pulled into a hospital room nearby.

She felt hands touching her brow, inspecting her limbs, and heard disembodied voices asking her questions... but

Alice couldn't pull her eyes from the ever-so-slowly closing doorway that separated her from that nightmarish scene she'd just witnessed.

"**AUS, BARBIE! AUS! PLATZ!!**" Matt ordered angrily, trying to subdue his extremely effective partner. They fired not one shot. The only shots fired were the ones the patient caused.

Not one person was dead... injuries? Yes.

But dead?

No, thank God, she thought, unable to pull her eyes from the door.

The dog's loud growling and ragged grunts from the effort of her scathing attack had ended—all that was left was the faint whimpering of a man who was truly in pain now... and that of the team moving into place to help and subdue him.

CHAPTER 10

Alice sat there trembling, propped on the side of the empty hospital bed. She'd stood up at one point but felt so lost, so off-kilter, that she'd steadied herself quickly, afraid to collapse. The horror of what she'd just gone through was still so fresh in her mind.

They were all safe.

Several nurses were sobbing in the room with her, still deathly afraid of what had just happened and the large animal outside the room that they'd seen actually savagely attack on command.

She had never heard Matt ever command the dog, and it was fascinating to hear the harsh sounding German words, but it was also incredible to watch how fast the dog obeyed. Barbie was terrifying in action—and it took years of training to make the two capable of responding to each other like that.

"Matt," she breathed fearfully as it finally sunk in that he was still out there, and her favorite duo had saved her. "Barbie…"

The door opened at that moment, revealing his anxious

face as he peered around the corner. The massive German Shepherd shoved past him, making some of the other nurses skitter away in fear… but not Alice.

"Oh, sweet girl," she whispered painfully, her heart breaking, as the dog immediately put her paws on either side of her on the bed and began whimpering as if the entire event scared her too.

Barbie was nuzzling her like she was one of her family.

"Sweet girl, I'm okay," Alice crooned, petting the animal and hugging her as the first tears began to fall. She choked back a sob as Matt walked over and wrapped his arms around her shoulders.

"Can everyone give us a few moments?" he asked politely over Alice's head. Once the room was cleared, he continued to hold her, cradling her, as Barbie continued to shove her nuzzle in between them, joining in on the group hug.

Barbie's tongue snaked out and licked her face where her head was angled downwards against Matt's chest, like she was curling up to hide. The acrid dog breath and the lick of the tongue made her jerk back immediately, half-sobbing… half-laughing.

"I think I just got French-kissed by your dog," Alice muttered, wiping her face as she straightened up, running the back of her hand across her mouth.

"Lucky mutt," Matt teased, ruffling the dog's ears playfully.

Alice looked up at him and saw the broken, shiny gaze that met her own. He'd been scared too.

"Are you okay?" he asked softly, his hand reaching for her. His warm hands ran over her cheeks, smoothing her hair, and came to rest on her shoulders. "I know how terrifying this must have been… but I swear I would let no one harm you. I came as fast as I could."

"I'm a little shaken up," Alice admitted shakily, nodding.

"Probably need therapy for years seeing this big girl in action," she teased, patting Barbie and scratching her muzzle, "... but I'm okay."

They both stood there for several moments, silent.

Alice knew keenly that she was still struggling internally somewhat... either that, or she just wanted to be held by Matt again. She needed to feel his arms around her, grounding her, and making her feel safe.

This was all new to her, and she wasn't sure how to ask without sounding too forward—but he seemed to thrive on the outlandish and outrageous, so she took a deep breath and spoke.

"Can you hold me again?" she whispered painfully.

Matt cursed softly and pulled her into his arms tightly, kissing the top of her head several times.

"Always, angel," he mumbled. "I will always be here for you."

Alice felt that mental wall she'd been trying to be strong behind crumble like a house of cards. She wasn't a weak or shy girl, but this entire event had her shaken like never before. That, and she'd never had someone like Matt in her life—who acted like he treasured her very presence.

She wrapped her arms around his middle and buried her face into his neck, ignoring the bits of his uniform that seemed to poke at her.

"I know this is crazy..." he began softly, smoothing her hair, "... and it's been a very crazy night, but are we still on for brunch? The full moon is bringing out all the reckless-ness in people—myself included."

Alice let out a nervous laugh and backed out of his embrace just enough to look up at him quizzically.

"I'm serious," he smiled.

"Only you could think about food at a time like this," she

admonished playfully. "Yes, we are still on for brunch—but I'm sure I look a mess so I'll have to…"

"You look utterly enchanting," he whispered, caressing her cheek.

Her eyes held his.

She wanted to pinch herself at the emotion in those brown eyes that looked at her unflinchingly, his soul bare before her. His finger slipped under her chin, angling her up just a smidgeon more, as his eyes dropped to her lips.

"Have I mentioned that people are crazy and reckless?"

"Yes—and I tend to agree," Alice breathed, unable to take her eyes off of him.

"So, you could forgive me if I am about to speak out of turn—and we could just blame it on the full moon, if I'm out of line?"

Alice swallowed shakily, not moving.

"I was so scared tonight when I saw you," he began. "It was like having my world snap into focus right before my eyes—and I realized I was just floundering around before, but I know what I need now…"

He hesitated.

"You," he uttered, his voice full of emotion. "I need you, Alice. I've never been in love before and never felt like this, but I can't go another day without saying the words."

Her breath caught in her chest as his thumb brushed over her lips, a silent promise that he would be kissing her soon.

"I love you—and I would stare down a hundred gunmen compared to how scared I feel right now, saying those three little words to you. I know how fast this all is… but it feels so right."

She opened her mouth to speak, and he shook his head.

"No," he interrupted. "I just wanted to tell you and you don't…"

"I love you, too," she uttered softly, touching his beloved face.

"I never believed in 'love at first sight' or any of that stuff… but when this handsome policeman literally fell into my world, spouting off the most outrageous things, and can cook better than me?" she teased tearfully, smiling up at him openly, her heart on her sleeve.

"What's a girl to do?"

A tear slipped from Matt's eyes as he smiled down at her.

"Well, for starters," he replied in a thick, exaggerated voice. "She should be kissing him senseless, you know? What kind of 'damsel in distress' doesn't know that she's supposed to start making out with the hero who rescues her?"

Alice laughed as he crushed his lips against hers. He kissed her deeply for several moments before cupping her face in his hands and breaking the kiss.

"I just French-kissed my girl after my dog…" he whispered, chuckling. "I must be completely head-over-heels for you, woman, because I've seen what Barbie licks when she thinks no one is looking."

Alice made a face.

"You are disgusting," she chuckled, laying her hands on his, where they rested on either side of her face.

"Yep," he grinned. "But you can't back out now. You love me and you can't unring that bell, angel. You're mine and I will always be yours."

He suddenly grew serious, causing Alice's smile to falter for a moment.

"Still feeling crazy?" he asked shakily.

"Sure," she breathed, smiling at him. "Why not?"

"Marry me," he whispered passionately. "It's completely insane, but I…"

The old-Alice would have frozen or balked immediately. She would have had to make a list of all the pluses and minuses, analyzed the best course of action, planned dates, and organized the entire thing... but since she met Matt?

Everything was crazy chaotic—but full of laughter and love.

He was a treasure and would always cherish her—because he had from the very first moment he'd laid eyes on her. She wasn't about to let him slip from her fingers, and whatever happens?

Well, they would figure it out somehow amidst crazy, scandalous jokes, kisses, and lots of laughter.

She couldn't ask for better!

"Yes," she breathed softly.

"I hope you know we are both calling in sick tomorrow," he teased, kissing her tenderly in relief. "Might call in sick on Monday, too."

"Deathly ill and have to stay home, right?" she uttered emphatically between kisses.

"Smart and beautiful," he sighed happily. "I'm a very lucky man indeed."

"I was just thinking the same thing," she admitted, feeling his lips smile against hers.

"Don't make me carry you out of here on my shoulder again, love," he teased, smiling, and then grew serious. "I've gotta pick up Grams or she won't make the cannolis—and she will seriously tan my hide."

"I think she likes tanned men, remember?"

"She does," he confirmed, grinning.

"Besides, maybe we can have cannolis at Christmas and on our anniversary from now on... we could start a new tradition," she smiled shyly, feeling so much love for him.

"That's it!" he quipped, backing away and startling Alice... but only for a split-second. He immediately swung her up in his arms before him and kissed her emphatically.

"Hang on, baby," he said tenderly. "We're getting hitched."

Alice wrapped her arms around his neck without question.

Matt practically strutted out the door. A man with a purpose. He hollered proudly, announcing it to the world, his voice booming with joy.

"We're getting married!"

She laughed happily as he carried her straight from the emergency room amidst catcalls, congratulations, and rounds of clapping hands.

ALICE STOOD before the judge at the courthouse and ignored the curious looks all around her. Other people were there to get married, dressed in their finest, wearing suits and dresses… even a few in what looked like ballgowns or embellished wedding attire with sequined patches placed on a white dress.

Not them.

Alice was still in her scrubs, spotted with blood from the ordeal earlier. Matt was in his police uniform…. and Grams was in her muumuu.

She smiled as she met the other woman's eyes, remembering her words fondly from less than an hour ago when they'd picked her up in a police cruiser, lights flashing wildly.

"Boy! 'Bout time you told her you love her! You've been mooning over her for a month now. Get my house shoes, Barbie! We are leaving now before you let her get out of your clutches…" the older woman ordered emphatically.

Barbie had bolted for one room at the back of the house as directed by the five-foot-tall tyrant that they all adored. The woman yanked a silken handkerchief out of a drawer, muttering under her breath as she tied it around her head to protect her hair.

"Finally decides to marry the girl and wakes me up at the crack of dawn to go to the courthouse. I don't even have my curlers out yet, and I'll be darned if we dally around for me to look fitting for this miracle. Nope! If I have to go there as bare as the day I was born, we are leaving right now…"

Alice smothered a laugh behind her hands at the memory.

Matt smiled.

"I love you," he uttered softly. "… and I sure love your smile."

The judge looked at them both, smiled, and sat back in his chair.

"Are you two finally ready to start, or should I give you a few moments?"

"I've been waiting for him my whole life," Alice replied honestly, beaming at the love in Matt's eyes as he smiled proudly.

"I think she's made me wait long enough," Matt answered, winking at Alice.

They both knew this was a whirlwind love affair for the ages, and both were going on sheer instinct, a hope, and a prayer, but whatever came? They could handle it together, because of one thing…

Love.

EPILOGUE

Fifteen years later...

"Hannah, can you help Grams with the sweet potatoes? Matt, don't you dare let your grandmother pull that turkey from the oven," Alice ordered from the dining room as she admired the full house.

Their eldest child, Hannah, was in a mood because she wanted to go over to a friend's house for Thanksgiving and there was no way any member of the family was going to spend the holiday away from them.

Tradition was tradition.

Period.

"Jamie, can you change Emily's diaper please—and no griping."

"Awww, mom," their ten-year-old son whined, rolling his eyes.

Alice almost smiled because he was the spitting image of Matt when he did that. Anytime Matt had wanted out of something, or protested, he rolled his eyes, stomped his foot, and huffed in frustration... right before he tried to distract her.

Five children later—he still did the same thing.

Alice met Matt's loving eyes as he winked at her, realizing the same thing she did. She wagged a finger at him playfully before pointing at the oven.

"Grams, step aside or my wife is going to put me on the couch again," Matt ordered with a mocking, fearful tone in his voice. He quickly smiled and then addressed their oldest son. "Jamie—get your sister's diaper please and do what your mother says."

"Yes, sir," came the begrudging response.

"Boy, don't you ever lie to me," his grandmother snarled, snapping a kitchen towel at him and making Matt jump at the sting. He looked at her wide-eyed, rubbing his backside.

"Owww, Grams. That *actually* stung."

"You know as well as I do, you haven't spent one single night on the couch, because I'm surrounded by a bushel of little heathens," the older woman said grumpily, turning to smile at Alice indulgently. "...And another on the way."

"She's got you there, buster," Alice crowed in delight, laying her hand on her outstretched stomach.

"Mama! Mama! Did you see Grams swat at Daddy?" two little earnest, laughing faces emerged from under the table. "Barbie keeps licking us and she smells bad."

"She's a sweet- but gassy- lady. You're lucky she doesn't mind you two hoodlums patting her all day long," Alice teased affectionately.

Barbie had 'retired' from the force about five years ago and they were blessed to have her around still. Her muzzle was gray, her teeth were starting to fall out, but she was as big a softie as ever before... she had been their family's protector from day one and adored the children.

"I thought you two were doing the utensils," Grams growled playfully, swirling the towel again in preparation for another swat...

Peals of laughter rang out as the house was full of mischief. The ninety-year-old woman was practically chasing her twin eight-year-old children around the table, while Jamie was angrily muttering about *'poopy diapers'* and *'how his parents were kissing and having babies all the time'*...

Matt had pulled the turkey from the stove and set it on top, walking over to join her.

"Mission accomplished, love."

"Thank you."

"How are you feeling?"

"Like a whale..." Alice admitted, smiling at him.

"You look utterly gorgeous, and I enjoy seeing you like this," he whispered secretly in her ear, dropping a soft kiss on her cheek. Alice arched her neck to allow him easier access to kiss her again.

"Like what?" she breathed.

"Full of yet another one of our beautiful babies," Matt replied tenderly, rubbing her lower back. She'd been complaining about it quite a bit, but still had almost a month to go before her due date. "You sure make beautiful children, Mrs. Jackson."

"I might say the same to you, Officer Jackson."

"It's sergeant now..." he grinned.

"Thank goodness, because with a sixth child on the way, it's getting pretty expensive to raise them," she admitted honestly.

"Soccer on Mondays, band practice almost every evening after school—plus competition on Saturdays... then we have tumbling for the twins on Wednesday evening. I have to tell you, *husband*... you are going to have to 'take one' for the team. I can't keep up with everything."

"Tell me what you need, and you know I'll happily give it to you," he said suggestively, wrapping his arms around her burgeoning middle and kissing her neck.

"Good," Alice grinned evilly. "You can start by teaching Hannah to drive."

Matt stood up and paled.

Their teenage daughter, who was setting the sweet potatoes on the table, instantly broke out in triumphant screams, dancing around happily, hugging them both.

"You are *soooo* going to pay for that," Matt breathed, swallowing hard. "I don't know that I'm ready for her to be driving."

"It's a rite of passage…" Alice grinned. "And if I am going to be 'passing' another child through this body—you can teach our eldest to drive."

Matt nodded, frowning.

Alice smiled, kissing him quickly and patting him on the cheek.

"Love you, Sergeant," she whispered fondly, teasing him. "Even more than the first day I met you, too. I think you've finally grown on me."

Matt got this lecherous leer on his face as he buried it in her hair, near her ear, whispering softly to her. Alice blushed fiercely. His grandmother hooted with laughter before she swatted Matt on the rear again with a kitchen towel.

"None of that, you two! The food is almost ready."

"I love you, angel," Matt said openly, winking at Alice. "We can finish our discussion tonight."

"We'll see," she said playfully, smiling back at him.

They had been blessed repeatedly over the years, falling more and more in love with each other every day. Sure, they had to suffer through hard times together…

It was knowing that they had each other, that they could make each other smile, and reveling in their love that gave them the strength to get through anything life threw at them.

Life, and their marriage, certainly hadn't been boring and if she had to do it all over again…?

She would have met him that very first Sunday for brunch, instead of making him wait... just so she could fall in love with Matt a little bit sooner.

DISASTER CITY SEARCH AND RESCUE SERIES

The Whirlwind Rescue

The Royal Rescue

The Jilted Bride Rescue

The Oil Tycoon Rescue

The Daring Rescue

The Widow Rescue

The Curvy Girl Rescue

The Rebel's Rescue

The Accidental Girlfriend Rescue

FLYBOYS

Discover a new series of exciting Heroes... Flyboys!

Flyboys are a group of men who thrive on adrenaline, toy with playboy reputations, and a bunch of self-proclaimed misfits. This sweet romantic series is full of soaring emotions, sweeping intense moments, and loyal friendships that unite the most unlikely characters into an unforgettable love story.

ABOUT THE AUTHOR

Ginny Sterling is a Texas transplant living in Kentucky. She spends her free time (Ha!) writing, quilting, and spending time with her husband and two children. Ginny can be reached on Facebook, Instagram, Twitter or via email at GinnySterlingBooks@gmail.com

Subscribe now to my Newsletter for updates

Made in the USA
Columbia, SC
22 May 2022